Blood Over Black Creek

Only 20,000 acres in size Black Creek was, by Texas standards, a small ranch but it had water in abundance. Its massive and powerful neighbour, the Bar-T ranch, claimed almost 400,000 acres of land but in summer its ranges usually ran dry. So protected by gunmen, its ranch hands constantly drove herds across Black Creek range to the water-rich creek which gave the little ranch its name.

Then Matt Crowe purchased Black Creek. A former outlaw, hired gun and bounty hunter, Crowe had never looked for trouble. He didn't have to for since the Civil War, it had always found him. Black Creek, with two sassy and very attractive twin sisters already in residence, proved to be no exception.

Yet what could one man and two beautiful young women do against the twenty hired gunmen of the mighty Bar-T? Very little – until Crowe found an old foe who became a dangerous ally. Then together their death-dealing six-guns turned the crystal clear waters of Black Creek blood red.

D1356249

By the same author

Rowdy's Raiders
Rowdy's Return
The Barfly
Dead Man's Boots
The Avengers of San Pedro
Across the Rio Grande
The Fastest Gun in Texas

Blood Over Black Creek

Edwin Derek

A Black Horse Western

ROBERT HALE

© Edwin Derek 2016
First published in Great Britain 2016

ISBN 978-0-7198-2066-3

The Crowood Press
The Stable Block
Crowood Lane
Ramsbury
Marlborough
Wiltshire SN8 2HR

www.bhwesterns.com

Robert Hale is an imprint
of The Crowood Press

Typeset by
Derek Doyle & Associates, Shaw Heath
Printed and bound in Great Britain by
CPI Group (UK) Ltd, Croydon, CR0 4YY

1

REUNION AT ROCKSPRING

Rockspring, Texas, west of the Pecos River.

It was a quiet and unusually hot spring day. Fortunately the porch in front of his office sheltered Sheriff Ben Foley from the worst of the sun's heat.

Rockspring hadn't always been this peaceful. Originally a Spanish settlement it had seen several melees as Mexico successfully won its independence from Spain and there had been more fighting when Texas had fought a bitter battle for its independence from Mexico. However, that and the Civil War were history. In the present the sheriff had more relevant problems to concern him.

'Sheriff, you look worried, is anything wrong?' asked his young deputy as he handed him an overdue mug of coffee. Ben grimaced as he sipped it.

'Yes, Willard. Apart from your terrible coffee, a dry spring means there will be no water on the Bar-T ranch this summer.'

'But there's always plenty of water on the Black Creek ranch,' protested the young deputy.

'Sure, but legally the Bar-T doesn't own Black Creek.'

'Maybe, but nobody round here is going to stop them driving their cattle across Black Creek land to the water. Besides, its owner, Bartholomew Trench, has already hired twenty gunmen to protect his ranch hands when they drive their cattle to the creek,' said the deputy.

'So Willard, you believe that nobody can stop the Bar-T?' asked Ben.

'I do. Even if enough top gunslingers could be hired to go against the Bar-T who would want to?' asked Willard.

'Nobody. Most town folk rely on the Bar-T for their livelihood. In fact, I can only think of two who don't,' said Ben.

'That would be Ma Cooper, she won't serve anyone connected with the Bar-T, and the other is Tom Johnston, the owner of the Liberty Stables, even though his brother Sirus is the Bar-T's lawyer. But none of them have enough money to hire a gunman capable of stopping the Bar-T,' said Willard.

'Then why is one of the two men I know to be capable of stopping them riding down High Street right now?' said Ben grimly.

Heading slowly towards them was a man Ben had once called friend.

He wore all black except around the edge of the crown of his Stetson was a solid silver hat ring. He rode a copper-coloured, roan stallion that seemed to move only below

6

the knees, giving its fortunate rider an almost jolt-free ride. Ben knew that it was a breed rarely seen outside Tennessee.

Bad memories of the time he had spent in that state during the Civil War flooded back into his mind. However, it was neither those memories nor the stallion that troubled Ben the most; it was the stallion's rider.

He loosened the tie holding back the hair pin trigger of his six-gun. Yet he knew that it would make no difference. Although there were still only a few faster on the draw than the veteran lawman, the man now tethering the copper roan was unarguably one of them.

'Shall I ask the stranger what business he has here?' asked his young deputy.

'Not if you want to live long enough to see this evening's sunset,' Ben replied grimly. 'Be a good lad and brew up some fresh coffee. The stranger takes it strong, very sweet and black.'

Clearly the man approaching them was no stranger to the sheriff, thought Willard, but before he could ask any questions the sheriff continued.

'Willard, listen to me carefully. When you return make sure you keep your gun-hand well away from your six-gun at all times. Your ma would never forgive me if I let anything happen to you.'

Mystified by Ben's remarks, the young deputy did as he was instructed and disappeared inside the sheriff's office just as the stranger reached the porch.

'Been a long time, Ben,' he said slowly.

'True, Major, but as trouble seems to follow you wherever you go, maybe it hasn't been long enough,' replied the sheriff.

Far from being offended, the stranger chuckled.

'True but it's been even longer since anyone called me Major, old friend. You know, whatever has happened to us since the war, you were far and away the best master sergeant to serve under me.'

'Flattery will get you nowhere except the worst cup of coffee this side of the Pecos River,' said Ben as the young deputy returned with a mug brimming over with coffee.

'Thank you, Deputy. Been a long ride and that reminds me, Ben, can you recommend a good stable? My horse has cast a shoe.'

'Is that why he was walking so oddly?' asked Willard.

'No,' laughed the stranger as he gingerly sipped his coffee. 'They breed them like that back where I come from, that's why they're called Tennessee Walkers.'

'Willard, take Major Crowe's horse up to the smithy – the Liberty Stable mind, not the one belonging to the Bar-T. Unless, of course, Matt, you've signed on for them?'

'No, I haven't. Done finished hiring out my gun and chasing "wanted men".'

Willard's face went white with shock.

'You're not *the* Matt Crowe,' he gasped.

'One and the same,' admitted the stranger, 'but don't let that worry you, like I say, my gun is no longer for hire. By the way, my horse's name is Geronimo on account he can outstay any band of troops of the United States Cavalry and outrun any sheriff's posse. Speak softly and treat him gently and then he won't give you any trouble.'

Willard walked slowly towards the tethered stallion and

then muttered something indistinguishable to him as he took the great steed's reins. Geronimo whinnied in response and then followed quietly after the young deputy.

As soon as he was out of earshot, Matt looked quizzically at the sheriff.

'Willard's an unusual name, Ben. Only come across it once.'

'You've still only come across it once. Martha runs a homestead a few miles out of town. Since Bill was shot she ekes out a living supplying the townsfolk with eggs, goat's milk, cheese and other bits and bobs.'

'So what happened to quarter-master Bill Smith?'

'Killed. Bushwhacked out on the range about just over a year ago. I've been looking out for Willard and Martha ever since.'

'Any idea who killed him?'

'Hell yes. Used to be a peaceful county until Bartholomew Trench bought up the Bar-T. You might have thought a four hundred thousand acre ranch was enough land for anybody but it seems it's not enough for Trench. Bill refused to sell his homestead and those who oppose the Bar-T don't live long.'

'Any proof that Trench was responsible?'

'There were two witnesses but they are dead too. Like I say, it doesn't pay to stand against the Bar-T.'

'Yet they have not moved against Martha and the homestead since.'

'No. Like I say, I sort of took her under my wing and so far Trench has respected that. But I guess that is only because he has another property on his mind.'

'What property?' asked Matt.

'Black Creek. I have no proof that Trench had any-thing to do with the death of Joe Wilson, its owner. He was a good old Texas boy and as straight as they come. He too refused to sell out to the Bar-T. Then, for some unexplainable reason his buggy overturned and the fall broke his neck. Of course, it may have been an accident but his death and that of the only other two witnesses to Bill Smith's death conveniently eliminated the men who stood in the way of the Bar-T extension plans. Mighty suspicious though the deaths were, without hard proof against Trench there was nothing I could do.'

'So why would Trench want Black Creek?' asked Matt.

'Even in the driest summer that little ranch has enough water for the entire Bar-T herd. Trench acts as if he owns all the range and Black Creek as well but I know that he doesn't. However, he has too many hired guns for anyone to challenge his claim to the range and as long as the real owners of Black Creek don't show up, there won't be any trouble.'

'Can the law not stop them?' asked Matt.

'Meaning me? No, I don't have the resources. Besides, most of the good people of Rockspring depend in some way upon the Bar-T for their livelihood. So they would soon vote any sheriff out of his office if he antagonized Trench.'

'But you wouldn't oppose the new owner of the Black Creek upholding his rights.'

'I doubt that the little help I could give would make much difference. Unless the new owner is lightning fast on the draw and has a natural instinct for survival, my guess is that he would be dead inside a week.'

'And if the owner had both of those things?'

'Then, Major Crowe, providing he had gunmen to back him up we would have a range war on our hands. But why do you ask?'

Matt reached into his pocket, pulled out a document and gave it to the sheriff. It was the deed to the Black Creek ranch and although it contained a number of complicated codicils relating to its actual ownership, clearly marked on it was the name of its new owner, Matt Crowe.

If Ben's worst fears had been realized, he didn't show it.

'So how come you bought Black Creek?' he asked.

'A bigwig in the bank that held the mortgage on Black Creek was a personal friend of the Governor. He thought the Governor might want to buy a little spread like Black Creek for when he retired but he intends to run for office again and told me about the ranch instead.

'You see, after he had granted me a pardon he asked me, unofficially of course, to rid him of a band of gun runners. Their base was in Mexico just south of the Rio Grande where neither the Rangers nor his State Troopers could officially operate.

'I rounded up a few good men and hunted down the gun runners. Then, when I returned he told me about Black Creek. My request to buy it was backed by the Governor so the bank let me have it for a fraction of what it's really worth. However, one of the conditions was they get a quarter of the proceeds from the sale of the next four herds we drive to Dodge or any other railhead town.'

'Sounds like a good deal for everybody concerned,'

said Ben admiringly.

'Perhaps, but there is a catch. Each herd we sell must not be less than one thousand head. If it is then I have to make good the difference. Also the cattle cannot be sold for less than ten cents per pound for every pound that each of them weighs. Again, if we have to sell below that figure I have to make up the difference. Finally the four cattle drives must be completed within five years or the bank reclaims Black Creek. In that event the bank would be entitled to all monies I had received from the herds already sold and I would be left with nothing.'

'Ouch! The bank can't lose; their people seem to have covered every angle.'

'True, but if I can pull it off I'll be able to make a real home on my own little ranch.'

'Black Creek has water to spare no matter how dry the summer gets and some of the best pasture land in this part of Texas. But Matt, what do you know about ranching?'

'Only what I picked up when I was working as a hired gun for a couple of ranches down by the Rio Grande. That said, the nearest I got to a steer was a cooked steak or a roast on Sunday. But didn't you once work on a ranch?'

'Sure did. Before the war when I was sixteen I hired on as a wrangler. In those days the cattle drives went up the old Shawnee Trail to St Louis. I did two more as a fully fledged drover before the Civil War broke out and ended the cattle trade for its duration.'

'Well, Ben. If you ever get tired of being a sheriff, I will be in need of a top hand so there will always be a job

12

waiting for you at Black Creek.'

'Thank you Matt, but I guess these old bones of mine have got too used to sleeping in a soft bed. Besides, like I said to young Willard, it looks as if we're set for a long, hot and dry summer. In that case, the Bar-T will stop at nothing to get to your water and as Trench wants your ranch he ain't likely to let you get a herd together.'

'In which case, I will have to stop them using my water,' said Matt.

'If you have the hired guns to back your play that will mean a range war,' said Ben grimly.

'You can relax Ben. I haven't any gunmen and I don't intend to start a range war.'

'Maybe not, Major, but then, doesn't the Good Book say something about the road to hell being paved with good intentions?'

Matt Crowe laughed and then grimaced as he drank his coffee. It wasn't the worst he had tasted but it was not far off it.

'Range war or not, you're right about one thing, some-body has to teach young Willard how to make decent coffee. In the meantime, where's the best place to stay and get a good hot bath?'

'It's round-up time so it's quiet in town at the moment. The Alhambra saloon is bound to have a few spare rooms. They don't do food and their whiskey is lousy. On the plus side, their saloon girls will have plenty of time on their hands until the Bar-T round-up is done. There's only six of them but they are all good-lookers. So if you're still interested in that sort of thing, the Alhambra isn't all bad news.'

'Maybe later but for now is there anywhere quieter?' asked Matt.

'Ma Cooper's. She only has a couple of rooms spare so I guess her place is too small to be called a hotel. It ain't cheap but it's always clean and it's by far the best food in town. I eat there every Sunday after morning church. Mind, she's fussy who stays under her roof but she's a friend of mind, so I'll have a word with her if you like.'

'Appreciate that, Ben.'

'Don't mean to pry but it's my job to ask, how long do you intend to stay in town before going to Black Creek?'

'Geronimo has to be reshod. I guess his hoof is bruised so he will probably need to rest for a day or two before I can ride him again.'

'Well, be warned, you might get a surprise or two when you get to your new ranch. On the other hand, is there any chance you might decide to sell out to the Bar-T? Given your reputation with a six-gun I'd bet Trench would be more than willing to take over your deal with the bank and still make it worth your while to sell. So why not sell it? After all, you did just say that you have no hands-on experience of running a ranch.'

'Ben, if I did sell out, what happens to Martha and her homestead?'

'In spite of everything I do to help out, I can't be every-where at once. Sooner or later Trench would burn the homestead to the ground.'

'In that case, Ben, you already know my answer.'

Matt Crowe then departed to get a beer at the Alhambra. Ben had been right, it was very quiet and its unoccupied girls were quite pretty. However, as he was covered in trail grime and smelt like the horse he had been riding, they didn't bother him.

Meanwhile, Ben went to make arrangements for his old friend to stay with Ma Cooper. On his way he ran into Willard as the young deputy returned from the Liberty stables.

'Is Mr Crowe staying?' he asked.

'Yep and for good. He's bought Black Creek,' Ben replied.

'I guess that means big trouble. But have you told him about the two girls at Black Creek?' asked Willard.

'Nope. You would have to go a long way to find two such sassy and pretty girls. So I figure it's better he finds that out for himself,' chuckled Ben.

'I'd like to see his face when he does,' said Willard, smiling broadly.

2

DEATH OF A GUNMAN

Unused to the luxury of a hot bath and a soft bed he had overslept and not awakened until the aroma of cooking bacon had drifted into his bedroom. So he hastily changed into his only other clothes, although they were old and rather shabby, fastened on his six-gun belt and then made his way to the dining room. Ben had been right; Ma Cooper was a fine cook and he ate a hearty breakfast although he spent most of it haggling with her over the price of doing his laundry.

Consequently, it was not until mid morning that he made his way to the stables to check on Geronimo. Tom Johnston, the smithy, had already reshod the Tennessee Walker. The big copper roan stallion apart from appearing to be a little unsettled seemed fine.

On his way back to Ma Cooper's, Matt dropped in at

the sheriff's office only to find that Ben had been called away on urgent business. As he left his old friend's office he became aware of a confrontation outside the hardware store. Young Willard seemed to have bitten off more than he could chew and was rapidly getting into serious trouble.

Parked outside the hardware store was a small and decrepit-looking buggy. It had apparently been driven to town by a very attractive, raven-haired young woman whose eyes were cornflower blue. Two gunmen barred her entry into the store but young Willard was trying to make them move aside. However, to no avail. Indeed, as Matt neared the scene it appeared the gunmen were trying to goad him into what would have been a very one-sided gunfight.

'Black Creek whores ain't allowed to buy supplies in this town any more and that's by order of the Bar-T.'

Anger blazed from the girl's startling blue eyes at the gunman's unsavoury comments, but the young and woefully inexperienced deputy intervened before she could respond.

'I represent the law around here, not the Bar-T, and I'll thank you to keep a civil tongue in your head when referring to Miss Wilson. As to the other matter, if her credit is good she is entitled to shop in the store,' said Willard firmly.

That only evoked hoots of derision from the gunmen.

'The Bar-T runs things round here, not some lame-brain deputy hardly old enough to shave, let alone tote a gun. But since you are wearing one, you're going to have to use it or get out of town.'

It was clear to Matt that unless he intervened the young deputy was about to get himself killed.

'Good morning, Deputy. Good morning Miss Wilson, pleased to make your acquaintance. Mind if I jump the queue? I need to get some ammunition from the store before I ride to Black Creek.'

Matt's remarks were deliberately calculated to turn the gunmen's attention away from young Willard. However, hearing the name of her home mentioned, it was Miss Wilson who turned her head sharply. However, in spite of her good looks Matt completely disregarded her. Matt only had eyes for the two gunmen.

'Stranger, don't go poking your nose where it ain't wanted,' growled the other gunman. 'You ain't going into the store and you sure as hell ain't going to hire out to the Black Creek ranch.'

The two gunmen looked at Matt's shabby town clothes and thought he must pose little threat. They should have been more observant and noticed the very professional way Matt wore his six-gun and how much more relaxed Willard had become since his intervention. Miss Wilson on the other hand did notice the latter although she had no idea why Willard had suddenly begun to smile. She was about to find out.

'I think you will find that I am going to do both those things. Now, stop this nonsense, step aside and be about your business, you're done here.'

The two gunmen instantly squared up to Matt. To them he was merely a temporary nuisance; a nobody whose fate would serve as another example to anyone else who defied the Bar-T.

Recognizing the inevitable, Matt spoke sharply to young Willard.

'Deputy, your duty is to get Miss Wilson out of harm's way. I'll deal with these two; this is Black Creek business.'

Unlike the gunmen who had not realized with whom they were dealing, Willard was too much in awe of Matt's fearsome reputation to argue. So he bustled the bewildered Miss Wilson to the other side of the street where they could watch the proceedings in relative safety.

Still the two Bar-T gunmen did not recognize the perilous position they were now in.

'Giving out orders, telling us what to; who do you think you are – Matt Crowe?' said the first gunman as he went for his six-gun. They were the last things he said and did.

'I don't *think* I'm Crowe, I *am* Matt Crowe,' said Matt as he drew. But the first Bar-T gunman didn't hear him for so swift was Matt's draw the luckless man was dead before Matt finished speaking.

Such was his prowess with the six-gun that even against two professional gunfighters, Matt was in no danger. His second bullet smashed the second gunman's shoulder before he had time to finish his draw. The force of the Peacemaker's bullet spun the hapless man round and he crashed to the ground, seriously but not fatally wounded.

In his long career as a top gunman, Matt had seldom been so merciful and mercy was not his motivation now. If the second gunman was lucky to still be alive it was only because Matt wanted him, when patched up, to deliver a warning to the Bar-T ranch.

Unaware of Matt's plan, Miss Wilson actually thought Matt was going to shoot the wounded gunman again as he lay groaning on the ground. Of course, she was wrong; Matt merely relieved him of his six-gun, looked at it in disgust, emptied it and then threw it on the ground. He then went over to the dead gunman, looked at his gun then removed its ammunition and put it in his own coat pocket.

'Willard, would you be so kind as to inform the under-taker there's one to be buried and I guess the other gunman could use the services of a doctor. When he's patched up, send him and both bills with my compliments to the Bar-T and make sure he takes this message with him; don't meddle in Black Creek business.'

'Consider it all done,' said Willard instantly.

Matt then turned to Willard's companion.

'Miss Wilson, I believe we both have business in the store. May I escort you there?'

'How can you be so cold-blooded and calm when you've just killed a man?' she said accusingly. Nevertheless, she took his arm and walked across the street with him.

'Miss Wilson, those men don't deserve your concern. They would have killed young Willard if I hadn't inter-vened. Besides, I only killed one of them. You see I'm not quite as bad as you seem to believe. I only kill when there isn't any other option.'

'You've killed before. Dare I ask how many?' she asked as they entered the store.

'If you include those killed by my actions during the Civil War, then I've lost count,' he replied truthfully.

'I doubt that you have a conscience but does that fact not bother you? Surely there must be some you regret killing?' she said coldly.

'Only one death I blame myself for and not a day passing that I don't regret my actions back then,' he said bitterly.

'Just one. You surprise me,' she said coldly. 'But how did you ever get started in such a violent way of life?'

'I guess it began in the war – I fought for the Confederacy. Afterwards, being a senior field officer I did not receive a pardon. So I became the target for several bounty hunters and lawmen. They gave me little choice. In fact, the choice was theirs; they didn't have to come after me nor did they have to reach for their six-guns when they finally found me.'

They were now at the counter. With a reluctance that both surprised and shocked her, she slowly relinquished his arm.

'Miss Wilson, let me assure you that the terrible events that occurred outside were not of this store's making and we are most happy to serve anyone from the Black Creek ranch,' interrupted the counter clerk, who appeared to have rehearsed his rather glib speech.

Matt thought that there was something vaguely familiar about him but as he took Miss Wilson's order, the clerk gave no sign of recognition. Matt noticed that her order was very small, covering only the essential supplies needed to keep a ranch going for no more than a couple of weeks.

Before the meagre supplies could be being loaded on to her wagon, the clerk addressed Miss Wilson hesitantly although his verbose speech again seemed well rehearsed.

'I regret having to bring this subject up in the presence

of a stranger, however expert he is with a six-gun, but I must point out that Black Creek is well over its agreed credit figure. I am not going to cave in to the demands of the Bar-T to not serve you again so I am not going cut off your supplies. However, I am a businessman and for my own salvation there are financial limits beyond which I dare not go, so a little on account before you require any more supplies would be appreciated.'

'Mr Bridger, you have been more than generous to us. I'm sorry I cannot make you any promises, as we too are owed money. As soon as we receive it I will settle the account in full.'

'How much would ease the situation?' asked Matt.

'That's none of your business,' retorted Miss Wilson sharply.

'That may be so,' said Bridger, 'but if this gentleman wishes to assist he would be helping me to help you. So if he has twenty dollars to spare. . . .'

In spite of the purchase of Black Creek, the deal Matt had cut with the bank meant that he was by no means a poor man. Not knowing what might be needed at Black Creek he had taken the precaution of bringing a substantial amount of cash with him. He put twenty dollars of it on the counter.

'I need a box of ammunition for my old Winchester carbine and another for my Peacemaker. Put the rest of the money against the outstanding Black Creek account and then have the full amount still outstanding made up into a bill.'

'What sort of girl do you think I am?' retorted Miss Wilson angrily. 'I will not take charity from a stranger especially when he's such a cold-blooded killer.'

'He's far from that, Miss Wilson.' It was Sheriff Foley. He had returned from his foray on to the range, which had been a wild goose chase.

'But . . .' was all Miss Wilson was able to say before the sheriff firmly interrupted her.

'Both of you in my office as soon as you've finished here. That's an order not a request. You're not going to give me any trouble over that, are you Matt?'

'No, my old friend. We will be finished here in just a few minutes and although Miss Wilson thinks I'm a wicked gun-toting ogre, perhaps when our business is done here she will condescend to accompany me to your office.'

From the way he spoke she could not help but think that in spite of her first impressions, Matt was an educated man. She was intrigued and despite her harsh words, she found that she didn't mind accompanying him at all. Indeed, she found no objection to taking his proffered arm as soon as they finished their store business. It was only a short walk and all too soon she was obliged to relinquish his arm as a few minutes later she found herself sitting in the sheriff's office, sipping quite palatable coffee.

'After this morning's events I thought it better to send young Willard home,' said the sheriff.

'Why? He did nothing wrong, in fact he was most gallant,' said Miss Wilson.

'Damn near got himself killed being gallant, as you call it. If he had died it would have been my fault. Not for the first time I'm greatly indebted to you, Matt.'

Matt shrugged his shoulders and said nothing. However, Miss Wilson was full of questions. Yet still more than a little afraid of Matt, she addressed them all to the sheriff.

'I don't understand what's been going on. Please explain, Sheriff Foley.'

'Of course. That's why I asked you here. To start with, my trip into the county was nothing more than a diversion to get me away from Rockspring so the Bar-T gunmen could goad Willard into a gunfight. Stopping you getting supplies gave them the perfect opportunity. Then, with the boy dead and buried, I guess Trench hoped Martha would be more inclined to sell her homestead.'

'I guessed as much,' said Matt.

'But Sheriff, why would this cold-blooded killer risk his life for someone he didn't know?' asked Miss Wilson, referring to Matt.

'Because Willard's late father served under him in the Civil War as did I,' replied Ben.

'But that still doesn't explain why he paid off part of Black Creek's arrears even after I said I wouldn't accept his charity,' she said in a puzzled voice.

'Over to you Matt, I'm not explaining that one.'

'I wondered if you'd remember that I was also in your office,' chuckled Matt.

'After this morning's shootings I could hardly forget that,' she replied sharply.

'Miss Wilson, I'm afraid there's no easy way to tell you. . . .'

'Tell me what?' she snapped angrily.

As she turned to face him, her beauty took Matt's

breath away.

'I am the new owner of Black Creek. I have the documents to prove it.'

'I don't believe you,' she said defiantly.

Matt fished the deeds of the ranch out of his pocket and passed them to her. As she read them her face turned ashen.

Ben then began to explain what had happened.

'Although you rightly regarded Jeremiah Wilson as your father, legally he wasn't. He and his wife took you in after your own parents were killed by an Indian war party. But I guess you already knew that.'

'Of course, Sheriff. Pa told us that as soon as he thought we were old enough to understand. But it made no difference, he was always *my* father.'

'Quite right, Faith,' said Ben. 'However, after his wife died of the fever, I guess you must have been twelve or so then, and as good a man as Jeremiah was, he proved to have no head for paperwork. Nor did he have any time for lawyers or any legal nonsense, as he used to call it. So he never legally adopted you.'

'I don't understand what difference that makes,' said Faith.

'Practically none around here,' replied the sheriff. 'Indeed most folks, including Bartholomew Trench, assumed that Black Creek was yours by right. And so it might have been, had your father not mortgaged your ranch and then defaulted on the payments.'

'But we were going to pay the bank when we got the money we are owed,' Faith protested.

'As far as the bank was concerned it wouldn't have

made any difference. As you were not legally adopted, in the eyes of the law you have no entitlement to Black Creek,' said the sheriff.

'You see, Miss Wilson, the bank were about to foreclose on your mortgage and take possession of your ranch. Through a friend, I got wind of it and did a deal with them. However, at the time I had no idea that you lived at Black Creek or I would have given you prior warning that I was coming to live there.'

'When will we have to move out?' she asked, her voice barely audible.

'Do you have anywhere to go?' he asked gently.

'No. It seems that you have achieved what the Bar-T has been trying to do ever since Pa died. Get us out of Black Creek.'

'You said we. Apart from yourself, who else lives at the ranch?'

'My sister. She's actually my twin. There's no one else except old Walt, he's the only hired help the Bar-T gunmen haven't scared off. But he doesn't normally live at the ranch. Only sometimes when we need an especially early start he sleeps over in the bunkhouse,' she replied.

Matt looked disbelievingly at Ben but he only smiled and then merely nodded his head in confirmation.

'Of course, we have had help from time to time, especially during the round-up. We had a decent-sized herd before the Bar-T branded most of our cattle as their own. Although the last time Walt checked we still had a few dozen left,' she added hastily.

It was Matt's turn to look ashen, but he recovered quickly.

'Tell me about the actual ranch house,' he asked.

As Miss Wilson began describing it, her face lit up. It was clear that she loved the ranch dearly.

'Parts of the ranch house are very old, dating back to when this land belonged to Mexico. At that time Indian war parties roamed freely across this land and as they had a habit of burning down settlements, a large water tank was built in the structure of its roof so there was always water on hand to put out any fires.'

Matt, fascinated by her enthusiasm and her detailed description of her home, was all agog to hear more.

'Filling the tank pail by pail must be a chore,' he said.

'We don't have to. Water is piped from one of the springs high up in the hills directly into the water tank. When it needs filling there are a number of valves and stopcocks you have to open and close in a special order. I don't really understand how it works, I only know that it does.'

Seeing the look of surprise on Matt's face, she continued.

'Upstairs, there's five full-size bedrooms and a proper bathroom. Downstairs there's a big main room and also a study, which we use to do all our accounts and paperwork. Then, of course, there is a kitchen, which is so large we not only use it for meals, we spend most of our time in it. Best of all is the view from our house. You can see right along the tree-lined river right down to our lake. It's truly breathtaking, especially in the fall.'

'The girls have lived there all their lives and have run the ranch almost single-handed since their pa died. Would have made a go of it too if it hadn't been for the

Bar-T,' said Ben ruefully.

'Well then,' said Matt. 'I offer you a difficult choice. You probably won't believe me when I say I'm not quite so cold-blooded as you think. So to prove it, I'll give you a few days to talk it over with your sister.'

'What choice?' asked Miss Wilson.

As she fought to keep the tears from her eyes, Matt's heart went out to her.

'Miss Wilson. If sharing your home with someone you think of only as a cold-blooded killer is not to your taste, you and your sister can leave any time you wish. However, I have a better idea.'

'And that is?' In spite of her best efforts tears streamed from her eyes. Matt desperately wanted to take her in his arms and comfort her but he found that he could not.

'As it's been your home all your life, why not stay? If you do, then you have my word that I will have a new deed of ownership drawn up giving you and your sister each ten per cent of Black Creek. To give you a little more security of tenure, I will also ensure that you and your sister have the power of attorney over any possible sale.'

Puzzled by Matt's last remarks, Miss Wilson turned and looked helplessly at the sheriff.

'I think he's trying to say that if you agree to stay, Black Creek can then only be sold if both you and your sister agree to the sale,' the lawman said reassuringly.

'There must be a catch. What would you want in return?' she asked between sobs, which she could no longer stifle.

'There's no catch, Miss Wilson. What I'm offering is nothing more than a good business deal for me. I've done

28

many things in my life, but ranching isn't one of them. So I need someone I can trust to run it and prevent me from making too many wrong decisions.'

'Well, if you put it that way, Mr Crowe, it all sounds quite reasonable. Of course, I must talk it over with my sister. There is one other thing. In spite of what you may have heard those dreadful Bar-T gunmen call me, both my sister and I try to be as respectable as any women running a ranch can be. So what sleeping arrangements will you require?'

'That will be entirely up to you, although perhaps it would be best for you to remain where you are; I could sleep in the bunkhouse.'

For some reason quite beyond her understanding, she found his answer disappointing – especially when Ben added, 'Matt Crowe is an honourable man. Too much so in my opinion for it has led to a long-running feud between two very good men whom I was once proud to call my friends. If Matt says he will sleep in the bunkhouse, then I assure you he will.'

Unless he is invited to sleep somewhere a whole lot more inviting, thought Miss Wilson. But that disreputable thought she kept to herself. She had the beginnings of an idea so preposterous she wasn't even going to share it with her beloved sister, from whom she had never before kept a single secret. However, her disreputable reverie was broken as an anxious-looking Bridger entered the sheriff's office.

'We haven't overloaded your buggy, Miss Wilson, but it looks as if the axle and one of its wheels have broken.'

She gasped in dismay at yet another setback. It had

been a bad day; two Bar-T gunmen had refused to let her enter the store to buy much-needed provisions and that had led to a gunfight and a man being killed almost in front of her. Then she had found out she had been an unwitting pawn in a plot to kill Willard. Worst of all, a notorious gun-hawk had purchased her ranch and now she could not get the supplies back to Black Creek without first having her buggy fixed, but she had no money for the repairs. What else could happen to her on this traumatic day?

3

THE TRAIL TO BLACK CREEK

The damage to the buggy was severe. Not only had the axle shaft sheared but several spokes in one of its wheels were shattered. Indeed, so bad was it that without costly repairs there was absolutely no chance of getting the buggy and the vital supplies it was carrying back to Black Creek.

Ben at once sent for the town's smithy, Tom Johnson. He proved to be a genial giant of a man, perhaps in his mid to late forties. Unfortunately, he only confirmed their worst fears.

'I can repair the buggy but frankly, you would be better buying another one. Of course, finding one for sale might not be that easy; there's not a lot of call for buggies in Rockspring.'

'I couldn't afford to buy one anyway,' said Miss Wilson

31

sadly, forgetting that she and her sister were no longer in charge of Black Creek.

'In any case, we need something bigger and sturdier,' said Matt.

'Well, I've got an old army wagon you can have,' offered Tom. 'It's quite small for a wagon and a bit run-down looking but if I grease the wheels and axles, even fully loaded it will get you back to Black Creek. Then, when you're next in Rockspring I'll give it a thorough overhaul.'

'I know the one, but it really needs two horses to pull it. Miss Faith's old hack wouldn't be able to pull it on its own,' said Ben.

'Do you have anything suitable I could buy?' asked Matt.

'I have as fine a pair of carthorses as you will find round these parts. Took them in lieu of payment for a job I did for dear old Bill Smith. He got killed before he could settle up so I've been keeping them against the time when Martha can pay me back. Even so, there's no legal reason why I couldn't sell them to you. However, the Bar-T would sure be riled if I did. No telling what they might do.'

'I quite understand, I guess it would be bad for business if you upset the Bar-T. In any case you would have to wait for payment,' said Faith Wilson sadly.

'You think I'm afraid of the Bar-T?' scoffed Tom. 'Besides, they got their own stables the other side of town so I don't get any of their work. I got no love for Trench or the way his gunslingers are trying to take over every-thing.'

'So will you help us? I can't afford to pay you until we get paid the money we're due.'

'Keep your money in your purse, Miss Wilson. Your pa and me were always good friends so you can borrow the wagon and have the use of the horses for free. They need the exercise and I'm sick and tired of feeding them. Got to be the greediest pair of carthorses in Texas!'

'But won't that upset the Bar-T even more?' asked Miss Wilson.

'I sure hope so,' chuckled Tom. 'Now don't you go worrying about me, Miss Wilson. I'm not foolish enough to carry a pistol so can't be goaded into a shoot-out. Besides, I got Susie to protect me while I'm working in the smithy and a shed load of Sharps buffalo rifles besides. They don't belong to me, but when the time comes, which after the gunplay this morning I'm sure it will, just remember they're Black Creek's for the asking,' said Tom.

There was no more deadly weapon than the incredibly powerful Sharps buffalo rifle, which if aimed accurately could kill a buffalo eight hundred yards away. In comparison, at eight hundred yards, the impact from a Winchester carbine would be no more deadly to a buffalo than a hornet's sting. Matt was about to ask how many buffalo rifles Tom had when he was forestalled by Miss Wilson.

'Who's Susie?' she asked.

'Best a fine lady like you don't know,' chuckled Tom.

Tom said that it would take him about an hour to get the army wagon ready to roll. Then, of course, it still had to be loaded with the supplies Miss Wilson had purchased from the store. Although there were not that many, they still had to be removed from the broken buggy.

Matt guessed his delightful female companion had not eaten that day. So, wishing for more of her company, he asked her to have lunch with him at Ma Cooper's even though he was not really that hungry after eating such a hearty breakfast.

Matt was right. In order to make an early start, she had forgone breakfast. Nevertheless, she declined his offer. However, Matt was so charmingly persistent he changed her mind. She rationalized her decision by saying that it would be some time before they would be able to start their journey back to Black Creek and it would be dusk before they reached the ranch. Even then, the wagon would have to be unloaded and the horses tended to before she could think about eating.

Ma Cooper was in her usual crotchety mood when they requested lunch.

'Don't normally do a cooked lunch but you can have a steak, beans and a couple of eggs to go with it for a dollar each in advance, if you please.'

Matt paid up before his charming companion could object. The steaks were huge and each of them was topped by three not two eggs.

'By all accounts you've had a bad day, Missy, and it's a fair old journey to Black Creek. So let old Ma Cooper feed you up a little. You can have my special apple pie and cream for afters, for free. Take your time and then by the time you've finished lunch I'll have Mr Crowe's laundry ready for him. But don't be bringing those clothes you're wearing for me to wash young man; one good scrub and they will fall apart.'

At this Faith Wilson burst out laughing. When she was happy her face lit up and her cornflower blue eyes seemed to shine. Matt thought she was by far the most beautiful woman he had ever met.

'Miss Wilson, do you think your sister will want to stay at the ranch?' he asked, really meaning did *she* want to stay at Black Creek.

'You will have to ask Rebecca that yourself, Mr Crowe, I wouldn't make the decision for her. The question is do you really want us to stay?'

'Yes, Miss Wilson, I do. Would it help to make up your mind if I went on one knee and begged you to stay?'

She laughed again and then became serious.

'I'm sorry that I called you a cold-blooded killer.'

'Think nothing off it, Miss Wilson, I been called many worse things than that.'

'Thank you, but to atone for my unpardonable rudeness, will you not call me Faith?'

'I'd be honoured to do so, Miss Faith.'

That wasn't what she wanted, she thought to herself. Blushing deeply at her forwardness she needed to take several deep breaths before continuing.

'If you please, not Miss, just Faith.'

'Only if you call me Matt.'

'Agreed, I'd like to do that. Now, to answer the question you just asked me; of course I want to stay on at Black Creek. When you see the ranch you will understand why I never want to leave it. If it's of any help, I believe that my sister feels the same way but as I said, it's her decision although I might try and influence her a bit,' she said, blushing slightly.

Even though they had only just met, Matt couldn't stop the smile of pure pleasure spreading across his face and seeing that smile, nor could Faith prevent her heart beating a little faster.

It was mid afternoon when they eventually left Rockspring. Matt drove the old army wagon with Faith at his side. He used the excuse that Geronimo's hoof was still a little too sore for the copper roan Tennessee Walker to be ridden.

Although a little on the small side for carthorses the two mares, called Daisy and Maisy, pulled the lightly loaded wagon with consummate ease. It was just that they preferred to travel at little more than walking pace. Matt, enjoying every moment of Faith's company, saw no need to hurry them on.

Faith's mind was still in turmoil. Perhaps that was not so surprising since much had happened to her that day. However, it was the charm of her mysterious and hitherto frightening companion rather than the day's life-changing events that had unsettled her so much.

Matt was nothing like her preconceived idea of a cold-blooded gunslinger. Indeed, he proved to be excellent company and gentlemanly in demeanour; his offer to give both her and her sister ten per cent ownership of Black Creek was incredibly generous. Yet he had shot a man dead and seriously wounded another and seemed to think no more of it than she would about swatting a horse fly. She found the contrast both alarming and intriguing. There were so many questions in her mind yet as they had only met a few hours ago, she dared not ask most of them. Nevertheless, she was determined to try to satisfy her curiosity as much as her sense of decency and decorum would allow.

'I heard someone call you Major,' she said as an opening.

'Yes, I once held that rank in the Confederate Army, although it seems a lifetime away now.'

'You must have been very young to hold such a high rank.'

'Perhaps. I graduated from West Point just before the Civil War began. In fact I was on leave, waiting for my first posting when war was declared.'

'Home was where? Or am I being too inquisitive?'

'Not at all. As I am taking over your ranch, it's not unreasonable that you would want to know something about me. My pa owned a small plantation in West Virginia. As the second son there was no chance of me inheriting it, so he sent me to West Point not just to be a soldier but to become an officer and a gentleman, as he used to put it.'

To Faith, Matt's demeanour made her believe he was both of those qualities.

'My uncle was a colonel in the Militia,' Matt continued. 'He was already staying with us when I came back from West Point. We all knew war was imminent and as he was recruiting officers I was happy to join up as a sub-lieutenant, even though it was the most junior rank of commissioned officer.'

'Were you not afraid of going to war?' asked Faith.

'No, although I should have been. I guess I was too young to realize what I was getting into. Looking back I was brash and altogether too full of myself then. Only later did I realize that the Militia was really nothing more than an independent cavalry unit, ill prepared for fighting on foot or the hand-to-hand combat that followed.'

'So what happened to change you?' asked Faith.

'As I said, we were soon in the thick of war and immediately incurred heavy casualties, especially among our senior officers. My uncle was killed in our first encounter with the enemy. After that, my promotions were probably as much to do with the deaths of my superior officers as my own ability.'

'So why didn't you return to your home after the war ended?'

'It was burnt down by Grant's army. My pa and elder brother were both killed. Not that I could have stayed there for any length of time. You see, after my uncle was killed, the Militia joined forces with Quantrill's marauders. By then, I had reached the rank of captain but later when Quantrill was also killed I was singled out by Anderson and on his direction I was promoted to major.'

'I have heard of both of them – they did some terrible things didn't they?'

'Yes, Faith, and I took part in some of them. War can do strange things to a man, but at least Anderson was a man of his word. But as an officer riding under his command, there was no armistice for me when the fighting stopped. On the contrary I became a "wanted man" with a reward on my head of initially two hundred dollars. So I moved west to Texas and hired my gun out to the big ranch owners, many of whom had supported the Confederacy. Unfortunately for me, most of them were replaced by Yankee carpetbaggers. So I became a bounty hunter amongst other things.'

At least one bad memory of the past still clearly haunted him but it was much too soon in their relationship for her to question him about it, so Faith changed the subject. To her surprise she found that she could talk about the morning's showdown without any feeling of unease.

'This morning, after the gunfight, you picked up both of the gunmen's Colts yet you only kept the bullets from one of them.'

'Because the other was an old forty-four calibre weapon called an "Army" Colt and it fires a different type of bullet to the one my Peacemaker uses.'

'I see. Matt, what do you intend to do with Black Creek?' she asked, fearing he might sell it to the Bar-T. His answer instantly reassured her.

'Try and make a go of it. But I'm no cowboy. Never roped a steer in my life so we need to hire some hands.'

How easily his name now came to her lips and she liked the way he had started to say 'we' when referring to Black Creek. Her mind returned to her scandalous thoughts about their future sleeping arrangements but she dare not say anything on that subject. Instead, she raised obvious objections to his plan.

'I doubt that Trench and his Bar-T gunmen would let us sign on any help and even if they did, where would we get the money to pay their wages? We are owed money but until the Jeffersons' herd reaches Dodge they won't be able to pay us.'

'The Jeffersons? I briefly met a family of that name when I was working for the Governor,' said Matt.

She desperately wanted to ask how a gunman with a price on his head came to be working for the Governor of Texas but her courage failed her. Instead, she continued to talk about the Jeffersons.

'Mr Jefferson is a distant cousin of the Governor. So possibly it is the same man. Anyway, he runs a ranch in the next county. I went to school with their daughter and when he heard that the Bar-T were branding our cattle Mr Jefferson offered to take the few of those that were left to Dodge with his herd. They left a few weeks ago.'

'So it will be at least a couple of months before the herd reaches Dodge and you get paid, but why didn't the Bar-T try and stop the Jeffersons moving your cattle?'

'Apart from being related to the Governor, the Jefferson family are all Quakers. It's well known that none of his men carry guns and not even the Bar-T would dare to attack unarmed cowboys. Besides Black Creek's contribution to the herd was only fifty head. I guess a number as small as that was probably not enough to worry Mr Trench, by all accounts he has thousands of cattle on his range.'

Matt did the sums. He may never have been a rancher but more than once he had been hired as a gunman by ranches at least as big as the Bar-T. So he knew about the sale of cattle.

His calculations proved that Faith was wrong about the value of Black Creek's little herd. At Dodge or any other railhead town, the price of beef was not usually less than ten cents a pound and when the seemingly insatiable demand back east exceeded supply, prices could almost double that figure.

Since a typical longhorn, even after the long trek northwards to Dodge, weighed about seven hundred pounds, each steer was worth a minimum of seventy dollars. Consequently, even the diminutive Black Creek herd was worth at least three-thousand five hundred dollars. As the steers had left before he had acquired Black Creek and were actually part of another ranch's herd, their sale was not part of the deal he had cut with the bank.

Nevertheless, Matt was concerned that the branding of Black Creek steers by the Bar-T, which in his eyes was rustling, might have reduced his stock so much he might not be able to meet the quota he needed to sell to satisfy his bank. However, preventing the Bar-T from branding any more of his steers would need several brave cowhands and at least one gunman equal to himself to protect them. But that was a problem for the future.

According to Faith, they were only just over halfway through the journey to Black Creek and the sun was already low in the sky. Faith thought her twin sister would worry about her if she didn't return by nightfall.

Reluctantly, for Matt had enjoyed Faith's company, he urged the two mares onwards. Even more reluctantly Daisy and Maisy broke into what can only be described as a gentle trot. However, they seemed capable of maintaining this leisurely pace as long as they were required to do so.

Although it was past mid-afternoon it was still very warm. Faith had been up since well before dawn and the day's events began to take their toll. That plus the gentle rocking as the wagon negotiated the well-worn trail began to lull her to sleep. Even her desire to find out why Matt, a wanted outlaw, had worked for the Governor took second place to the drowsiness which suddenly overcame her.

Indeed, she was so weary that without really realizing what she was doing she snuggled up to Matt, rested her head on his shoulder and promptly fell asleep. Grinning broadly, Matt put his arm around her shoulders. Of course, it was only to ensure Faith did not topple over and fall out of the wagon – or so he tried to convince himself.

Daisy and Maisy maintained their steady lope with consummate ease, although occasionally they needed a little prompting from Matt. Then, with Faith still asleep and just as the sun was beginning to set, they came to a fork in the trail. Matt reined in the mares although they were hardly blowing.

Should he stay on the main trail or take the fork? As there was nothing to indicate which one led to Black Creek, Matt had to wake Faith. He did it as gently as he could.

She woke smiling but that expression turned to dismay when she realized that she had snuggled so intimately into him.

'I'm so sorry, Matt. What must you think of me?' she cried as she quickly moved away.

'I think none the worse of you for falling asleep and leaning on my shoulder. I guess this has been a very long and difficult day for you. I didn't want to wake you but I had to know which trail to take.'

'Take the less used trail to your right. Drive slowly because it winds to and fro for the next mile or so but

42

we've almost reached Black Creek.'

She was correct. As the last rays of the sun began to die away they breasted a rise in the trail; Black Creek lay before them. The ranch house was actually situated near the north and dead end of a long and broad box canyon, which sloped downwards from north to south.

Northwards, the canyon ended in a range of black rocky crags. It was from the dark colour of these rocks and not the crystal clear water of the springs that fed the creek that the ranch derived the first part of its name.

In fact, due to a freak of nature, a multitude of springs emanated from the black crags. One of them disappeared from view as it plunged straight back into the hillside; the one that had been piped directly into the ranch house. The rest flowed down the canyon until they all joined together to form the creek, which was actually a stretch of fast-flowing crystal clear water. Even in this unusually dry spring the depth of the water was chest high. As it flowed further down the canyon the creek narrowed so much that the flow rate of its water increased until it became strong enough to sweep away anybody foolish enough to try to wade across at that point. However, perhaps another quarter of a mile down the box canyon the tree-lined creek widened to form a ford.

Matt was surprised to find that directly in front of them the trail divided. One, seemingly well used, led down to the ford while the other, less well used, swung northwards and led to the ranch house. Turning back towards the ford, from his elevated position, Matt could see that the creek eventually ran into the only sizable lake in this part of Texas.

43

Even in the now rapidly fading light Matt could see that around the lake and running on either side of the creek the ground was covered in acre after acre of lush grass, perfect for grazing cattle. No wonder the little Black Creek ranch was coveted by the mighty Bar-T. However, possibly due to their nefarious activities, there were surprisingly few cattle in sight.

The ranch house was actually located about three hundred yards from the edge of the creek and perhaps fifty feet or so above it. As they drew closer it appeared to be larger than he had imagined from Faith's earlier description.

Save for an open gateway the ranch house was completely surrounded by a chest high, white picket fence. Inside the sizable enclosure there was, apart from the actual house, a corral and a large barn. However, Matt could not see any sign of the bunkhouse in which he had agreed to sleep.

As darkness descended, the intensity of the light inside the ranch house seemed to increase. Standing on the porch, silhouetted by the light streaming out of the doorway behind her, Matt could see a young woman.

'Is that you, Faith?' she yelled.

'Yes darling. Sorry to be so late but it's been quite a day. By the way, I've got somebody with me.'

Then a grizzled old man appeared from behind the barn. He seemed to have a slight limp.

'It's all right Walt, everything is fine. Would you see to the horses? We seem to have got three new ones. Then, after you're done you can go home. We can leave unloading the wagon until the morning.'

'Very good, Miss Faith. Leave the mares to me, I know them well, they used to belong to the Smith family.'

'Leave my horse to me,' said Matt as he leapt down from the wagon and tethered Geronimo to the ranch house's hitching rail. Then, as Walt unhitched the two mares the smell of hot coffee began to fill the air.

Faith was met by a young woman who embraced her with a passionate yet sisterly hug; she was obviously Faith's twin sister although her hair was ripened-corn blonde. Otherwise her features and build were very similar to Faith's; they even possessed the same striking cornflower blue eyes.

'Sis, I was so worried about you,' said the blonde woman.

'Sorry, but I got unavoidably delayed,' replied Faith truthfully.

'So what's happened to our old buggy and who is the man at your side?' she said, pointing an accusing finger at Matt.

'Its wheel broke so I borrowed this wagon from Mr Johnson. The man by my side, as you so charmingly put it, is Matt and he's here to stay.'

'I don't understand.'

'Miss Rebecca, before explanations and at the risk of making the same sort of bad start as I did with your sister Faith this morning, I must insist that you promise never again to stand in front of a lighted doorway. You make a perfect target and I for one do not want to have to scrub your blood off the paintwork.'

'Since when did the hired help start giving out orders?' she retorted angrily. She was going to say more but a warning glance from Faith silenced her.

'Why don't I see to Geronimo and give you two ladies a chance to catch up on the news? And I'd love a cup of that delicious smelling coffee when I get back.'

'Geronimo, the Apache chief? That's a funny name for a horse – and why does he walk so oddly?'

'He walks that way because he's a breed known as a Tennessee Walker. As to his name, he's called Geronimo because he can outlast any cavalry troop and outrun any sheriff's posse,' said Matt as he went to see to his stallion.

Matt took his time so that Faith could relate at least some of the day's events. He slowly led Geronimo to the corral and then unsaddled him. He left his saddle, saddle bags and his carbine in the barn but kept hold of his shotgun and his money wallet. Then, he slowly returned to the ranch house. Waiting for him was a strong cup of sweet black coffee and a very perturbed young blonde woman, who in her own way was as attractive as her raven-haired sister.

'So you've bought our home,' she said accusingly.

'Yes, Miss Rebecca. However, your sister has said she will stay on and I hope you will as well.'

'Darling,' said Faith to her sister, 'so much has happened today I guess it's too much for you to take in all at once. We can discuss it later but for the moment let's start over again. This is Mr Crowe, Matt – this is my twin sister Rebecca.'

'Matt Crowe! Are you the infamous gunfighter?'

'Infamous! That's the first time I've been called that. Faith called me a cold-blooded killer when first we met this morning, but I think I like infamous better.'

46

'Yes, I did call him that,' said Faith. 'He is indeed Matt Crowe, hired gun, former outlaw and bounty hunter. Yet he isn't at all like the cold-blooded killer I took him to be, even though this morning he killed a man and wounded another right in front of me.'

'Maybe so, but this terrible gunfighter has purchased our ranch!'

'Yes dear, I've seen the deeds and the sheriff has verified them. As to the man he killed and the one he wounded, they both were Bar-T gunmen and would have killed Willard if Matt had not intervened.'

Her twin looked somewhat askance at Faith as her hitherto prim and rather proper sister used Matt's christian name.

'And I must correct you Miss Wilson,' he said grinning at the blonde-haired beauty in front of him. 'I'm not a terrible gunman. The fact that I am still alive after all these years is surely proof that I'm a pretty good one.'

At least his jest brought the semblance of a smile from Rebecca Wilson's lips. Matt thought she was a real beauty but he already knew that his heart was destined elsewhere.

After a rather fraught supper, Matt slept in the barn rather than the bunkhouse simply because he couldn't be bothered to look for it. Only later did he discover that it was tucked away directly behind the barn. However, sleeping in the barn was no hardship, its freshly-cut straw made a soft, warm and comfortable bed.

While Matt slept peacefully in the barn, the sisters talked long into the night. As Faith gave a detailed account of the day's events her full support of Matt's actions evinced further questions and then reproof from

47

her ever so slightly younger twin.

'Many times you have accused me of being too familiar in my conversations with the opposite sex. You have only known this gunman for only a few hours and yet you permit him to freely use your christian name and call him by his. What has happened to my prim and I have sometimes thought over-proper sister?'

Faith blushed profusely and then related how she had fallen asleep on Matt's shoulder during their homeward journey. At first her twin pretended to be shocked but keeping up the pretence proved to be beyond her and much to her Faith's consternation, her twin burst into peels of laughter.

'Faith,' said Becky when she eventually regained at least some control of herself, 'I cannot find fault in your actions – my only doubt is your choice of partner. On the other hand, in a sort of rugged way, I cannot deny he is a handsome man. Yet if you choose to be so free with your christian name with him then you cannot chastise me for doing the same. As to me remaining here, it's my home too so of course I will stay. Besides, I wouldn't dream of leaving you here alone with Mr Crowe.'

'Why not, Becky? Matt has given me his word that I'll be quite safe and Sheriff Foley has assured me that Matt is someone I can trust.'

'Even from the briefest of acquaintances I don't doubt that for a moment. But, I've seen the way you look at him, sister dear, so if I'm not here, who's going to protect Matt from you?'

Faith blushed deeply, evoking a great deal of merriment from Becky as she had several times been accused by her sister of being too familiar with the opposite sex.

Flustered and embarrassed and seeing that there was no more sense to be had from her sister that night, Faith retreated to the sanctuary of her bedroom.

4

GUNFIGHT AT THE BAR-T

There was much to do just to keep Black Creek ticking over although the girls, with a little help from Walt, had made huge improvements to the ranch house and its surrounding buildings. In broad daylight Matt could see that even the picket fence had been freshly painted white and both the barn and the bunkhouse behind it were in prime condition.

The ranch house had also received a great deal of attention. The adobe walls forming the oldest part had also recently been painted white while inside was spotlessly clean, neat and very tidy. It was clear to Matt that the girls had worked very hard. Indeed, according to what he had heard from Ben Foley, Black Creek had looked careworn and run-down until they had taken charge.

True to his word, the following day, Matt rode to

Rockspring and had the town's only legal man, Sirus Johnson, alter the deeds to the little ranch to give each twin ten per cent ownership of Black Creek.

Sirus was the younger half-brother of Tom Johnson. They shared the same father yet, except in one thing, there was little similarity between the brothers in either appearance or aptitude. Tom was a broad-shouldered giant of a man whilst Sirus was small, slim and wiry. Unusually for a lawyer and again completely unlike his brother, he always packed a six-gun.

The one thing in common the brothers did have was their hatred of Trench and everything he stood for. However, Sirus was not a man to let his feelings get in the way of his business and the Bar-T ranch account was his most important. Little did Matt realize how important this would prove to be.

Several days passed without incident, then on a routine patrol along the boundary with the Bar-T, Matt discovered a significant number of freshly branded Bar-T steers. It appeared that the steers had been herded together prior to being driven across Black Creek range to its lake.

Matt resolved to confront Trench. Faith was particularly vocal in her opposition to his plan but in spite of pleas from both girls, he still rode over to the Bar-T ranch. The trip was not quite as risky as the twins seemed to think because he expected most of their men, including the hired guns, to be engaged in the formation of the herd soon to be driven to Dodge.

In stark contrast to the verdant water-rich land surrounding Black Creek, the ground leading to the Bar-T was brown and barren even though it was still spring. The vista was only broken by cacti, some no higher than a man's waist while others as straight as telegraph poles reached skywards, although none as high as the gaunt windmill that pumped to the surface the only water to be found for miles.

As befitted a ranch of its size and importance, the Bar-T ranch house was huge and its bunkhouse was bigger than the barn and bunkhouse at Black Creek put together. Yet as Matt had expected, there were only a very few hands around as Geronimo trotted into its massive courtyard and most of those were Mexican. Luckily for Matt, it seemed that Trench had adopted a policy similar to the one used in many of the large Texas ranches for none of the Mexicans were armed.

However, one man leaning nonchalantly against the barn was armed. In fact, he toted two silver-pearl handled pistols. Unusually, both were butt-first in their ornately decorated brown leather holsters.

Expensively clad in flashy golden-brown buckskin, he had a scar running down the length of the right side of his face. Matt recognized him at once. The man called himself Sanchez and had featured in several 'Wanted Dead or Alive' posters Matt had kept during his days as a bounty hunter.

Matt was still wearing his old and rather shabby town clothes so it was perhaps not so surprising that the gunman hadn't recognized him. By the way he addressed Matt, it seemed Sanchez had mistaken him for a drifter.

'Don't dismount, we ain't hiring drifters today or any day soon, so turn your horse round and be off. You ain't wanted here.'

'Maybe not,' said Matt as he dismounted, disregarding the lone gunman's orders.

The well-trained Geronimo had been through similar situations so many times he didn't need orders to tell him what to do. Sanchez was standing on the opposite side of the courtyard only just within the range of most six-guns. So the Tennessee Walker quietly eased his way backwards until a signal from Matt indicated to the great stallion that he was safely out of six-gun range.

'I said be off with you,' shouted Sanchez angrily .

'Not until you agree to move your cattle off my land and keep them away,' said Matt firmly.

'And what land would that be?' asked the Bar-T gunman unpleasantly.

'Black Creek. Now, I'm not an unreasonable man and I realize it's still round-up time. But once it's over you are to remove the rest of your steers. If you don't, then any unbranded cattle left on my range will be considered the property of the Black Creek ranch.'

A somewhat portly, distinguished man, perhaps in his late forties, appeared at the ranch house main door. Clearly, he had heard Sanchez shouting and picked up enough of the conversation to realize what was happening. He too addressed Matt as if he were a no-account saddle-tramp.

'Listen you, I don't know what sort of riff-raff Black Creek is hiring these days but my name is Trench and I own the Bar-T. As this is your first time here I will give you this one warning to give to those two silly women who think they own Black Creek. Then, providing you quit that ranch and ride off immediately, never to return, you will not be harmed.'

'And this warning?' asked Matt calmly.

'Just this; the Bar-T lays claim to all the range within a day's ride from this ranch house.'

'Even Black Creek?' asked Matt.

'Especially Black Creek. Now, like yourself, I'm not an unreasonable man, so I want you to take those two silly girls another message; I am prepared to offer them ten cents an acre for their ranch. They have until the round-up is over and my herd is safely on its way to Dodge to accept my offer. But if they have not left Black Creek by then I will burn their little ranch house to the ground with them inside it. Do you understand?'

'I understand that you can try but as I have the deeds to Black Creek the law is surely on my side.'

'The only law around here is my law and I have twenty gunmen to enforce it,' retorted Trench angrily. 'As to any deeds, a single match will soon put an end to them. So stranger, you now know where you stand.'

'No, Trench. I only know where you stand and that's what I came to find out. Oh, by the way, yesterday in Rockspring I had a little run-in with some of your men, so now you have two less gunmen.'

Matt saw the frown grow on the face of Trench. Clearly, news of yesterday's gunfight had not yet reached him. Nevertheless the Bar-T ranch owner reacted quickly.

'This conversation is becoming a bore. Sanchez, deal with this fool.'

'My pleasure, Mr Trench,' he said as he reached for the butts of both of his six-guns.

So confident was the Bar-T owner of Sanchez's ability

to outdraw this outspoken saddle-tramp, he turned round and began to make his way back into the huge ranch house. However, he had barely reached its front door when two shots rang out in rapid succession. He naturally assumed they were from Sanchez's pair of six-guns and so turned round to congratulate his top gunman.

Trench was shocked at what he saw. The Bar-T's top gunman lay dead on the ground in front of the barn door. Because the distance between them was at the limit of the Peacemaker's range, Matt had fired twice. However, both bullets had hit their intended target.

'Don't shoot me, I'm not armed!' Trench cried out in panic.

'I didn't think you would be; your type hires others to do your dirty work. Not that I am in any position to judge; I've hired my gun out to men just like you,' said Matt bitterly.

At a signal from Matt, Geronimo obediently trotted to his master's side. Matt holstered his Peacemaker and then leapt athletically into his horse's saddle. For the moment there were only the unarmed Mexicans in the yard staring helplessly at the fallen Sanchez. However, the shots were bound to attract attention and the courtyard might soon be full of Bar-T gunmen.

'Who are you?' gasped Trench.

'Matt Crowe, the new owner of Black Creek and my order still stands; get your cattle off my land.'

Without waiting for a response Matt galloped rapidly away. However, had he stayed, he would have seen a smile of satisfaction spread slowly across Trench's face.

He hadn't become the owner of the Bar-T without

making a few very good contacts. He was also an intelligent, quick-witted but utterly ruthless man. To him the loss of Sanchez was merely a small inconvenience.

By the time he had reached his office he had already formed a plan to deal with Crowe. He sat down at his desk and in impeccable copperplate writing composed a letter to the one gunfighter who could not only successfully oppose Crowe but had held a bitter grudge against him for many years.

Within the hour, the letter was on its way to Rockspring. There, one of his underlings would have its contents transmitted via the telegraph to one of his contacts back east. A reliable man who had already arranged the hire of Trench's gunmen. For some reason, the latest gunman the owner of the Bar-T intended to hire was known to be a bitter enemy of Crowe and was reputed to be even faster on the draw.

Hiring so many gunmen was a severe drain on Bar-T's financial resources. However, the sale of its herd which by the end of the round-up was expected to rise to more than two thousand head would not only enable him to redeem its outstanding mortgage and pay all of the other debts but would also fund the launch of his political campaign to eventually become Governor of Texas. Then, when he needed more funds next year, there would be another herd to take the twelve hundred mile trail northwards to Dodge.

The only real obstacle to success had been the stubborn resistance of Black Creek; all-year-round access by Bar-T cattle to its never-ending supply of water was vital to his plans. For the moment Crowe posed a threat.

Nevertheless, Trench was confident that when he arrived, his new top gun would soon resolve that problem.

During the next few days, the Bar-T ranges were a hive of activity as their cowboys and gunmen joined forces to push the newly-branded cattle into a cohesive herd. So in groups of three or four they were driven to the banks of the only stream that ran across the vast ranges of the Bar-T. Unfortunately during the summer the stream usually ran dry but for the moment it provided enough water for the newly-assembled herd.

It took several days to achieve but its head count finally topped two thousand. So the trail drive began. However, not without incident. Right from the start the steers became widely scattered and it needed the extra help of the Bar-T's gunmen to assist the cowhands to keep the herd together. As a result, initially at least, progress was painfully slow. Indeed, it took the herd five days to cover the first dozen miles. Then a strange thing happened.

Unbidden by the cowhands and completely of their own accord, a few of the bolder steers took the lead and stayed there. As soon as they did a few more steers began to follow directly behind them – and then more followed directly behind them. The process of follow-my-leader took some time to complete but eventually the herd snaked back in a line as far as the eye could see. Yet the herd was never more than a few steers wide.

Although some of the gunmen were amazed at the change, they soon learned that was a normal thing for herds to do. It seems that sooner or later some sort of pecking order always occurred as the cattle made their way northwards along the long Western Trail to Dodge.

They also learnt that once the steers had settled their position in the line, stampedes excepted, they were unlikely to change it again, thus making it much easier for the cowhands to keep the herd moving.

Consequently, the gunmen were no longer needed. Indeed, their continued presence began to unsettle the steers. Nevertheless, they remained with the herd for several more days. Then, as Trench had ordered, at the rate of three per day, they began to return to the Bar-T.

The gunmen drew lots to decide the order in which they left the cattle drive. The first three chosen were delighted but had they known what fate had in store for them, they might have wished to remain with the herd until it reached Dodge.

5

ENTER JOHN WESLEY

Almost two hours before sunrise and while the first three gunmen to return to the Bar-T were still sleeping, Faith set out in the wagon for Rockspring. This time, much to her disappointment, Walt, not Matt, was her escort. They were going to settle the debt owed to Mr Bridger's hardware store and then purchase more supplies. All this was to be achieved with funds provided by Matt, who had arranged for some of the money earned during his bounty hunting days to be transferred to the small but safe bank in Rockspring.

Although Matt had amassed a tidy sum of money, he was not prepared to use all of it on Black Creek. He had another long-standing commitment that was a constant drain on his resources. It related to the one action in his life of which he was forever ashamed. In fact, the main reason he had purchased Black Creek was to more fully atone for his actions, or rather lack of them, so many years ago.

Breakfast, cooked by Becky, was a quiet affair. The presence of Matt, especially now he had returned to his all-black garb, had strangely affected her so for the most part she kept silent. For his part Matt was mulling over what more he could do to protect his ranch and the twins against Trench and the Bar-T gunmen.

On his own there was very little he could do; somehow he had to get help. But from where? He was trying to figure that out when a ragged fusillade of shots suddenly broke out although there seemed little need for concern as the shots were some distance away and there was no responding salvo.

Peace and quiet returned for a little while until another even more ragged volley was fired. Once again there was no return fire but this time Becky was concerned because the latest gunfire came from the southern edge of Black Creek's ranges and that was where she had seen the last of their steers grazing.

Although Matt was reluctant to leave Becky on her own, he felt he had to ride out and investigate the shootings. He secretly feared that in retaliation to his visit to the Bar-T, Trench might have ordered a couple of his hands to stampede the last of the Black Creek cattle on to the Bar-T range.

So leaving his fully-loaded shotgun with Becky, Matt saddled Geronimo. As the big stallion galloped away from the ranch house, more shots rang out. Yet they were still very distant and seemed no nearer to the ranch house than the very first shots.

Becky heard only one more round of shots fired after Matt left. Once again, there was no response to them. At first she too feared that Trench's henchmen were stampeding the last of the Black Creek herd but discounted the idea because of the intervals between the shots.

In happier times, before Trench had arrived on the scene, both twins had been allowed to ride with the Black Creek cowboys as they tended the cattle out on the range. As a result, Becky was well versed in the ways of handling steers and knew it only took a few unexpected shots to spook a herd into a stampede.

Once on the run, nothing could stop the steers until they had run themselves to a standstill, usually a distance of no more than three or four miles. Yet even that relatively short distance would have taken them onto Bar-T land; so there would have been no need for further shooting after the initial volley.

As time passed and Matt failed to return, Becky feared that he might have been lured into an ambush. Noon came and went and still there was no sign of Matt. She was beginning to panic when, in the distance, she saw a black-garbed rider mounted on a copper-coloured roan slowly approaching.

From behind the safety of the ranch windows' slatted shutters, Becky watched his approach with growing concern. At first, she thought she recognized the rider's unusual coloured roan; Matt rode one of similarly unusual hue so at first she thought it was him. However, as this roan approached she could see that its forelocks were much darker than Geronimo's. Otherwise the two roans were almost identical, even having the same unusual gait.

Although of generally similar appearance, the rider wasn't Matt. So fearing that the Bar-T had acquired a new gunman, she grabbed the already loaded double-barrelled shotgun Matt had left to cover such emergencies and then stepped outside.

'Hallo the house!' The lone rider called out the traditional greeting, reined in his copper-coloured roan and waited for a response.

'What do you want?' she said, pointing the shotgun at the stranger. Unfortunately, Matt's shotgun was much heavier than she thought and she found it difficult to keep its barrels level.

Fortunately the stranger didn't seem to notice her difficulty and addressed her in a calm and cultured fashion; his very slight drawl suggested he was from the south, although his choice of words was very odd.

'It's been a long ride so I need to water my horse at thy trough if I may,' he said as he dismounted.

Although Becky thought the stranger was handsome, his appearance scared her. A Mexican style gun-belt full of bullets hung diagonally from his left shoulder and joined a more normal gun-belt at his right hip. Yet that too had bullets in it. They were stored in ornate little pouches, which stretched all along his belt. She thought that combination of the belts together with their spare bullets must be very heavy.

Like Matt, he too wore a single six-gun low on his thigh. Becky instantly feared him although his smile seemed both genuine and utterly disarming.

Nevertheless, she kept the shotgun pointed at him even though she continued to struggle to hold its heavy barrels high enough to shoot the stranger.

'Ma'am, I guess thou art alone and I can see not used to wielding such a heavy weapon. Please lower it. Then, I shall give thee my pledge that no harm shall befall thee and thine family at my hand. Indeed, I will protect thee whilst thou art alone,' he said.

She had heard that strange mixture of old and modern languish once before. That had been when an Amish family briefly stopped over on their way to settle in New Mexico. But the stranger couldn't be Amish for their religion forbade the carrying or use of firearms and this stranger was even more heavily armed than Matt.

'Ma'am, although thy weapon is a powerful dangerous one at close quarters I must tell thee I am out of range. I am also afeared that if thou should fire then its recoil may do thee more damage than its buckshot to me. Therefore, be thou still whilst I prove I am not thine enemy.'

Raising his gun hand high above his head he reached into his saddlebag with his left hand and very slowly extracted a very unusual looking six-gun. Unusual because although it was clearly a Colt, its barrel was no more than half the length of the almost universally-used Peacemaker.

The stranger gently placed the short-barrelled Colt on the ground and then stepped away from it.

'With your permission I will walk my horse, Cochise, to the trough by your corral. While he's drinking please pick up my little six-gun, which has sometimes been called the Sheriff's Colt. It's loaded so take care. Please, I beseech thee; use it to defend thyself instead of that shotgun.'

As he walked Cochise away from her and towards the water trough he kept his gun hand on the roan's reins. Since he would then have to release the reins before turning a full one hundred and eighty degrees before he could draw his six-gun, Becky thought it would be safe to pick up the short-barrelled Colt.

She was quite wrong. The stranger was so fast on the draw he could have released the reins (Cochise had been well trained to remain stationary at such times), swivelled round, drawn and fired before her hand had even reached the little Colt.

But he didn't do any of those things. He had given his pledge that he would not harm her and to John Wesley, errant son of a preacher, a pledge was an oath never to be broken. So Becky safely picked up the short-barrelled Colt and gratefully placed the shotgun on the ground in front of her.

The barn door was open. Cochise having drunk as much as his master would permit, he whinnied with plea-sure as he saw mounds of freshly cut hay inside it.

'Ma'am, my Cochise has had nothing but wire grass and scrub these last five days. I'll gladly pay for all the hay he eats.'

'Your Tennessee Walker may eat as much as you permit him to. This is a Texas ranch, not a town stable. I will not profit from feeding a hungry horse however unusual his name. Now, I will trust you this far but no further. You must also be thirsty and after five days on the trail, you may wish to freshen up. Behind the barn is our old water pump, although it's no longer in regular use it still works perfectly and its water is still clear as crystal. So if you want to wash off the trail dust you can do so in perfect privacy.'

When he smiled he looked much younger, although maybe he was just a little too . . . Well, she couldn't quite explain what it was about him, even to herself. Yet whatever it was there was something about him that sent ice cold chills of fear running down her spine. There was no logic to it because although Matt was also a gunman the tingle that he sent running down her spine every time he smiled evoked an entirely different feeling. A feeling she dare not tell her sister about, for she was quite certain that Faith felt the same way about Matt.

'Thank you ma'am,' he said as he broke her train of thoughts. 'As to his name, I call him that because. . . .'

'He can outlast any cavalry troop and outrun any posse,' interrupted Becky.

'You took the words right out of my mouth,' he said.

As he began to lead Cochise to the barn he started to frown; there was only one way this otherwise charming young woman could have known what he was going to say. The fact that she had also seemed to recognize his horse merely strengthened his suspicion. Without realizing it he automatically undid the grip holding down the hair pin trigger of his Colt six-gun. There was only one other horse that looked like Cochise and that was his twin. Its rider, once his childhood friend was now his most bitter enemy. So, if his assumption was correct, he was certain he would have need of his Colt this day.

His assumption was only partly right, for it was not his long-time enemy he was soon to face. Instead, the challenge would come from the enemies of his enemy and taking up arms against them would change the course of his life forever.

Once Cochise had been fed and was safely tethered out of sight in the barn, the stranger made his way to the old water pump. He was surprised to see that almost hidden by the barn was a small bunkhouse and that although it was now empty, it had all the signs of recent occupation.

Although it was still spring, it was hot enough for his clothes to dry whilst still on him. As they needed a soaking even more than he did, he kept them on. So removing only his two gun-belts, six-gun and Stetson, he doused himself with water. Indeed, he enjoyed the feeling of the fresh cold water so much he repeated the process several times. Unfortunately, as he did so, the noise of the falling water drowned the sound of rapidly approaching riders, three in all.

Of course, Becky saw them. As they approached she realized that she had met them all before; they were Bar-T gunmen, scum of the worst kind, so she knew their intentions would not be friendly. Nevertheless, she waited in the courtyard, the short-barrelled Colt grasped tightly in her hand.

They arrived in a cloud of dust and dismounted simultaneously. Their leader spoke gloatingly.

'Well boys, the plan worked out fine. Here we are and Crowe is out on the plain chasing after the gun shots fired by the Mexicans. They were tickled pink to be allowed this once to carry firearms.'

'Does that mean we got time for having a little fun with this sassy minx?' asked one of the other gunmen.

'I don't see why not. She's always been a stuck-up little

bitch. Guess we got time to bring her down a peg or two. Mind, when we're done with her we have to get down to the real business we came to do. What say you boys?' the leader of the gunmen replied.

'Sure thing, I ain't proud so I'll take her after you've finished with her,' said the other gunman.

'Strip her naked and make her beg for it while I watch. Then, I'll be happy to go last and have my fun after you've both finished having yours,' said the third Bar-T gunman.

'Aren't you forgetting I've got a gun?' said Becky, trying to hide the fear she felt.

'Missy, from the way you are holding that little six-gun I guess you've never shot a man in cold blood. Well, now's the time to start. I ain't going to draw my six-gun in case I harm you. Instead, you and me are going to get down and party in the dirt.'

The Bar-T gunman was right; she couldn't bring herself to shoot him even when he approached her.

'There's a good little girl, drop the gun and then take off your skirt. You know boys, I think we got her all wrong; she's going to enjoy it as much as us. Now girlie, here's the deal, we going to have you whatever you do to try and stop us. But play nicely and when we've done here we will leave you to live another day. Otherwise, we will shut you in the barn while we burn it down. It's your choice.'

She dropped the pistol on to the ground, gritted her teeth and began to undo her skirt. There was nothing else she could do; she couldn't fight off all three of them.

The gunmen watched goggle-eyed as Becky's skirt slid to the ground. Underneath it she wore only a short white petticoat attached by buttons to her bodice. The petticoat was so short it revealed her knees – something that even saloon whores seldom did.

'That next,' gloated the leader of the gunmen as he pointed at her petticoat.

Stifling a sob Becky began to oblige. Slowly her trembling fingers began to undo the first of the buttons that held it to her bodice. The gunmen watched with such avid interest they failed to notice the still soaking-wet stranger as he began to quietly work his way behind the three Bar-T gunmen. Yet although his clothes were wet, his gun-belts and six-gun were all bone dry.

Becky noticed the stranger. She had not expected any help from him; to her he was or had been just another gunman. Nevertheless, now that she saw what he was trying to do, it gave her the strength to help him in the only way she could; by keeping the gunmen's attention solely focused on her.

She quickly undid the second button on her right. That part of her petticoat slipped a little further revealing more than a glimpse of her extremely shapely bare thigh. Just one more button should give the stranger time to get into position she thought – and she was correct. As more of her thigh and the top of her right leg came into view, the stranger at last interrupted the proceedings.

'That will be all for today boys; reach or draw,' he said.

Startled, all three gunmen whirled round reaching for their six-guns as they did so. But the stranger was far too experienced to stand directly behind them. Instead, as all the gunmen wore their six-guns on their right hip, he stood slightly to their left side as they turned round to face him.

Consequently, they had to sweep their six-guns from right to left across their bodies in order to aim and fire at him. None managed to do so. The stranger's first bullet hit the nearest gunman in the stomach. Instantly, he doubled up and grunting with pain, pitched face first on to the ground, his gun not even clearing its holster.

The stranger's second bullet struck the centre gunman full in the chest. Its force knocked him off his feet and he fell backwards. His six-gun had cleared its leather holster but he was dead before he could fire it.

As he spun round, the third gunman, their lippy leader, recognized the stranger instantly so made no attempt to draw. Instead, he threw his hands into the air and begged for mercy.

'Don't shoot, Captain Wesley! Don't shoot; I ain't going to draw against the likes of you.'

'Unbuckle your gun belt and then kick it away from you,' the black-garbed stranger said.

'Anything you say, Captain,' replied the crestfallen gunman who very carefully, so as not to risk being shot by mistake, undid his gun belt and then as it fell to the floor, immediately kicked it to one side.

'Ma'am, taking good care not to come between him and me would thou be so kind as to collect his gun belt, thy shotgun and my short-barrelled Colt. Please do it at once and then take them to the barn and leave them there. You can keep the Colt if you've a mind to,' he said as an afterthought.

Without stopping to do up her petticoat, she did as requested and then did only one of the buttons of her petticoat up. Quite deliberately, she left the others undone. Then, with the short-barrelled Colt grasped firmly in her hand she left the barn intending to confront the gunman who had so humiliated her.

He was a changed man now, so much so that the stranger had thought it safe to remove the six-gun from the gunman he had shot in the stomach. That Bar-T man was in such a bad way he was in no condition to resist.

Still revealing a glimpse of a very shapely thigh she confronted the hapless gunman.

'Not so bold now are you,' she scoffed.

The gunman made no reply.

'What do you want me to do with him?' asked the stranger.

'Nothing yet, there's something I want him to see first,' she said fiercely.

All sense of decorum and proper conduct had deserted her; she not only again undid the second button on the right side of her petticoat but also undid one on her left side.

'Have another glimpse of what you were after,' she said, as her heart pounded at an alarming rate.

Nonplussed the gunman stared at her.

Becky held the pose for a several seconds.

'Now it's your turn,' she said to the gunman.

'I don't understand,' he replied.

'I think the lady means it's your turn to remove your clothes,' said the stranger as he burst out laughing.

'But it ain't the same for a man,' protested the gunman.

'Last time I held a gun you said I wouldn't use it. After what you just put me through, do you still think so?' she said, ominously cocking the short-barrelled Colt.

Slowly the gunman took off his shirt, his boots and then his denims, leaving just his pink long johns. But then he hesitated.

'And the rest – all the rest,' she snapped.

Face ashen white with mortification and accompanied by the increasing groans of the wounded gunman still lying helpless on the ground, he did as he was ordered. A few seconds later he stood naked before them. But Becky hadn't finished with him yet.

'Stand with your legs apart,' she ordered.

Puzzled by the instruction the gunman complied. Puzzled that is until he realized what he thought Becky was going to do. Then fear flooded over him as she took careful aim at his manhood.

'Better hope the lady is a good shot,' the stranger said as he burst out laughing again.

'For pity's sake, not that,' the gunman begged.

'Do I have to pull this wiggly thing to make it work?' asked Becky innocently. (She was, of course, referring to the Colt's trigger.) 'You see I've never fired one of these before.'

The gunman's panic increased fourfold.

'Yes, take aim and then gently squeeze the trigger,' said the stranger, thoroughly enjoying the joke.

'Legs wider apart if you please, they're not what I'm aiming at,' said Becky coldly.

She fired with a far greater expertise than she had led them to believe. The bullet went safely between the gunman's legs, barely grazing one side of that appendage which men hold most dear. Nevertheless the gunman fell as if he had been struck by an axe. But he wasn't hurt. To compound his humiliation, he had only fainted.

Still half undressed, Becky collected up the gunman's clothes and hid them in the hay in the barn. While she did so the stranger helped the severely wounded gunman on to his horse, slapped its rear and sent it on its way. The horse trotted off in the general direction of the Bar-T ranch but although he didn't say so, John Wesley was certain its severely-wounded rider would be dead before it arrived.

Becky returned from the barn, still holding the little Colt. She made no attempt to do up the buttons on her petticoat as the still naked gunman came round. Becky wasn't done with him yet.

'Unsaddle your horse,' she snapped.

Whining pitifully, the naked gunman did as he was bade.

'Now you can ride him bare-back to the Bar-T,' she ordered.

'Have some mercy. Arriving at the Bar-T without my clothes will make me the laughing stock of the county,' he said, aghast at the prospect.

'I'm showing the same amount of mercy that you showed to me. Get on your horse and ride back to the Bar-T. Or next time I pull the trigger, I won't miss it, if you know what I mean.'

He knew exactly what Becky meant. However, the naked gunman found mounting an unsaddled horse with no stirrups to give him a footing was no easy task. To make matters worse, fearing that Becky would carry out her threat, the gunman desperately grabbed his horse's mane and then started to pull himself on to its back.

Startled by his rider's strange behaviour, the steed reared and the naked gunman fell to the ground. It took him two more attempts before he managed to climb on to the horse's back. He then rode off in a flurry of dust. Both Becky and the stranger burst into fits of laughter as he did so.

'Perhaps I'd better introduce myself,' he said as the laughter died down. 'My name is John Wesley.'

'I was christened Rebecca Emily Wilson, but taking into account what we've just been through and my disreputable attire, you can call me Becky.'

'My pleasure, Miss Becky. As to thine attire, perhaps I should turn my back while you button up your petticoat. I know I promised not to harm thee and I always try to keep my word but thou art an extremely comely young woman and even I have in my limits.'

'Good,' she said brazenly. 'I release you from your promise. No man has ever seen me in such a disreputable state let alone touched me. But while this wild mood still holds me in its grip you may kiss me if you want to.'

However, as she looked up she saw in the distance plumes of dust being kicked up by a horse or horses galloping towards the ranch house.

Seeing the look of alarm on her face, John turned. She saw the look of disappointment on his face as he too saw the dust plumes.

'I have to go back in the house, I don't want anybody else to see me like this. But will you not kiss me before I have to go? I may never be this wanton again.'

He kissed her lightly on the lips but it was not enough

for Becky. She quickly undid the top of her bodice and then grabbed his hand and pressed it hard on her right breast.

'You're the first to touch me,' she said as she gathered up her skirt before rushing into the ranch house. As she did so she thought to herself that she had admonished Faith for being too forward in letting Matt call her by her christian name on the first day that they had met. Yet that was nothing when compared to what she had just done.

The rapidly-nearing plumes of dust allowed John Wesley no time to dwell on Becky's astonishing change of attitude towards him. They had been caused by just one rider galloping frantically towards the ranch. Although he could not identify him, John no longer doubted the rider's identity. As he wasn't prepared to meet Matt Crowe out in the open until Becky had explained what had happened, he retreated into the barn and then reloaded his six-gun.

Fortunately, his stallion, Cochise, was still in the barn. The fine stallion was the twin of Geronimo, Matt's copper-coloured Tennessee Walker. It was bound to whinny a greeting to its twin, therefore confrontation with its rider was inevitable.

Not for one moment did John doubt his prowess with his six-gun. It was just that Crowe was one of the very few gunmen he knew to be at least as fast or even faster than he was. They had grown up together and as children they had been the best of friends. However, boys grow into men and their bitter feud dated back to the first days of the Civil War. So in spite of any explanation Becky might offer regarding the dead body lying in the courtyard and her dishevelled appearance, he didn't doubt that within the hour he would be put to the test. Then and only then would he finally discover who was the faster draw.

6

THE VENDETTA EXPLAINED

Matt rode into the courtyard, saw the dead body and fearing something terrible had happed to Becky, hastily dismounted. His fears were only partially assuaged as she came out of the ranch house. In haste she had re-dressed but in contrast to her usual neat and tidy appearance, she looked extremely dishevelled.

'I was on my way back to the ranch house when I heard shots. Then I rode as fast as I could. But are you all right? I can see there's a dead body yet the blood on the ground doesn't look if it came from him.'

'Yes, I'm fine now, but it was touch and go for a bit. You see there were three of them, if it hadn't been for Captain Wesley, I dread to think what would have happened.'

'Wesley!' exclaimed Matt.

'Yes, Matt. I am indeed here and right behind you. I've

got you covered with my carbine but I won't fire unless I have to in case the young lady gets hit by a stray bullet. I've given her my word that no harm shall come to her by my hand.'

'I know you to be a man of your word, John, so will you accept mine when I say I too will not put Becky at risk by drawing on you. So how about a coffee or two and maybe you would like to something to eat? For old time's sake, can we not act in a civilized manner before we face each other? I'd like to hear your version of what happened here.'

'And I'd like to know why the notorious Matt Crowe is a hired hand on this ranch? Or then again, if you will pardon the liberty, ma'am, if Miss Becky is the reason, you've been a lucky man. Unfortunately for you that luck has just run out. However, for Miss Becky's sake I agree to temporarily postpone our confrontation. You have my word on it.'

Further conversation was interrupted by the sudden arrival of Faith and Walt in the old army wagon, now loaded down with supplies. The three of them had been so wrapped up with the events in the courtyard they had failed to hear or even notice the approach of the wagon.

Faith gasped as she noticed her sister's extremely untidy appearance. Then saw the dead body lying on the ground, now surrounded by a swarm of flies. At first she recoiled in horror but recovered almost instantly and started to ask a barrage of questions.

'Sis, are you all right? What's been happening while I've been away? Who is the stranger standing by your side and who shot the dead man? What have you been doing to make your clothes so dishevelled? Who is this stranger and why is he all wet?' She asked all these questions without drawing breath.

'I'd like to know the answers to some of those questions too,' said Matt grimly.

'Miss Wilson, my name is John Wesley. As a stranger here it ill behoves me to give orders but the sight and smell of a dead body, especially when it is left in this heat, is a something that no young lady should have to endure. So may I suggest that it is removed with all due haste?'

'You're right of course, John. But then in most things you usually are,' said Matt.

'If I unload the wagon I could then take the body of this no-good Bar-T gunman to Sheriff Foley, but I ain't as young as I used to be, so I could use some help,' Walt added ruefully.

'You said the gunmen were from the Bar-T. I'm afraid that complicates things for me,' exclaimed John Wesley. 'Matt, I must beg for your indulgence in settling the issue between us. Shall we call a truce until noon tomorrow? There is much I need to know and maybe I have information that could be of some use to you.'

'John, I think if for no other reason than for the sake of the girls we should pool whatever information we have. Whatever you think of me now we were once good friends.'

'A dead Bar-T gunman; a stranger who says that he killed him and says the killing only complicates things for him and then there's talk of a truce between old friends! Fine! Since no one body seems to want to tell me what's going on, I'll go and cook us something. . . .'

Faith suddenly stopped speaking and as realization came to her, a look of horror spread over her face.

'Miss Faith, whatever is the matter?' asked John.

'Mr Wesley, please tell me that you have never met or even heard of our local sheriff, his name is Ben Foley,' she said.

'Sheriff you say. If he is the same master-sergeant who served Matt so well during the Civil War, then I am afraid I cannot deny knowing him. You see, Ben Foley and I go back a very long way. We were once staunch friends and even though he is now a sheriff and I'm a hired gun, I hope we still are. But why do you ask, has Ben ever mentioned me?'

'Not directly by name but something he said when I first met Matt made me afraid that you knew him.'

'Whatever did Sheriff Foley say?' asked Becky, whose turn it was to be baffled.

'Never you mind, Sis. Just go and collect some eggs and see if there are any mushrooms while you're about it. Then, while the men handle the chores outside I'll see what else I can rustle up for us to eat.'

As the men were about to leave, Faith interrupted their departure with another question.

'Walt, will you stay for a meal after the wagon has been emptied? You're more than welcome.'

'No Miss Faith. The sooner I get the body to the sheriff the better. After that, I'll get Ma Cooper to cook supper for me. The way she feels about the Bar-T she will be glad to do it after I've told her what's happened here.'

'Right then. Gentlemen, to your chores while Becky and I go about ours.'

Their chores completed, Walt set off for Rockspring. The seemingly tireless mares were making their third journey in twelve hours. Yet they pulled the old army wagon, albeit loaded only with the body of the Bar-T gunman, with so much ease it might have been their first outing of the day.

Matt and John Wesley were about to enter the ranch house when John hesitated. His peculiar sense of honour required that if he was not welcome in any house he would not enter it. Unless, of course, acting as a bounty hunter he was chasing after a 'wanted man'.

Whilst they had been unloading the wagon, Becky had returned with a basket full of eggs and wild button mushrooms. Sensing that John might feel uncomfortable about entering the ranch house after everything that had happened, she returned outside and then ushered him in. However, it was Faith who greeted John as they reached the kitchen table where he again hesitated.

'Sit down, Mr Wesley. I would not have the food I have prepared go to waste,' she said sternly.

Time, or lack of it, ensured the meal was only a simple repast. Nevertheless, the large plates full of belly pork, beans, mushrooms and fried eggs looked and tasted good, so it was no surprise that they were quickly devoured.

The meal was eaten in silence. Then, while Becky served coffee, Faith began to seek answers to the questions that had been bothering her since her return from Rockspring. First, she wanted to hear Becky's version of the events in the courtyard.

Only omitting her last indiscretion with John, Becky

described in graphic detail the afternoon's events. However, Faith, although deeply grateful for John's intervention was not satisfied; she wanted an explanation for John's sudden and unexpected appearance at the ranch.

'Mr or should I call you Captain Wesley, you have been described as an honourable man by Sheriff Foley and he is a man who is not prone to give such strong recommendations without good reason. So tell me truthfully, what is one of the most notorious gunmen in all of Texas doing on our little ranch?'

'Only notorious?' queried Matt. 'I got called infamous and a cold-blooded killer when I first arrived. By those standards John, it seems you've made a good impression.'

The laughter caused by his remarks did much to ease the tension around the table.

'Miss Faith, the Civil War is long gone so I no longer use my rank. As to my arrival at this ranch, it was not intended. I must admit to being a little off course,' admitted John.

'It was very fortunate for me that you were,' interrupted Becky. 'But that still doesn't explain why you are here in this part of the Texas Panhandle, does it?'

'No it doesn't. Normally I do not discuss my private or business affairs with anyone. However, as the reason I'm here clearly involves all of you, this one time I will make an exception.'

Hushed into silence by the sheer force of his personality, they waited with mounting anxiety for John Wesley to continue. But he did not. Instead he asked for another cup of coffee and then began to slowly sip it.

'Please continue Mr Wesley,' Faith said in a voice so ice

cold it caused Becky to turn her head sharply towards her sister.

'I'm here because I was responding to a letter from a Mr Trench of the Bar-T ranch. Fortunately, as it turned out, I accidentally ran across this little ranch without knowing its name. As it was very warm I decided to stop and ask for water for Cochise.'

'Mr Wesley, I can offer little excuse for prying into your affairs save that they might directly affect Black Creek, but I must beg you to tell us about the contents of your letter.'

'I believe that the contents of the letter may well affect Black Creek although Trench does not mention the ranch directly. However, before I continue I note that you call my old friend by his christian name. Is it too much to ask that both you and Miss Becky address me in a similar way?'

'That depends on what your intentions are, Mr Wesley,' replied Faith before Becky could reply in the affirmative.

'That seems perfectly reasonable, Miss Faith, although Miss Becky already knows that she and her loved ones are now under my personal protection. As Matt and your friend Ben Foley already know, once given, I never go back on my word.

'As to the letter, it contained an offer of a great deal of money to deal with a gunman hired by a small ranch in order to cause the Bar-T a great deal of trouble. He said the gunman in question was Matt Crowe, so how could I refuse?'

'And will you take up the offer?' asked Becky, horrified at the thought of a showdown between Matt and John.

'No, Miss Becky,' he replied and reverting to his

strange mixture of modern and olden speech continued, 'You see, I gave thee my word that I shall not harm thee or those thou hold dearest and at the risk of repeating myself, I always keep my word.

'But there was one other thing thou should knowest – in his letter Trench said that after I had dealt with Matt he would then take control of this ranch using whatever force he deemed necessary. He offered me even more money to lead his gunmen until Black Creek was utterly destroyed.'

'So what will you do?' asked Matt.

'As to the matter that stands between us, I have taken an oath of retribution on that. But after that, if you will have me, I will stand in place of Matt against the Bar-T.'

'Not so fast, Mr Wesley. First, I think you owe my sister and me an explanation for your vendetta against Matt,' said Faith sharply.

'Perhaps I do, but it is a deep and very personal matter so I can say no more,' said John.

'Then I will,' said Matt. 'It concerns John's sister, Anne. We grew up together and were almost like sister and brother. I say almost because as we got older it wasn't like a sister that I loved her and I know she came to feel the same way about me. So the night before we set off to the war. . . .'

Matt broke off, too overcome by his feelings of remorse to continue.

'So what happened to her?' asked Faith, her voice quivering with emotion.

'She died in childbirth, alone and in poverty, shunned by the rest of my family,' replied John bitterly.

'I swear I didn't know she had become pregnant,' said Matt sadly. 'I loved her dearly and I would have done everything within my power to return home and marry her before returning to my regiment.'

'And the child?' asked Becky.

'She lived,' said John. 'But even as a-babe-in arms my beloved and most religious family wanted as little as possible to do with their illegitimate granddaughter. So she was farmed out to a distant aunt of mine who agreed to look after her while she was an infant. But only for a price. So after the war was over I became a bounty hunter partly to pay for her upkeep. At first my scheme worked well but whilst I was in the Badlands tracking a wanted man, she mysteriously disappeared. In spite of my best efforts I lost track of her,' replied John bitterly.

'Again I'm to blame,' said Matt. 'Purely by chance, I discovered I had a daughter. Of course, I couldn't look after her myself so I arranged for her to live with someone I could trust, one of the West Point cadets I graduated with. Although he was born in Nelsonville his folks originally came from my home town and he served under me. During the war he married a schoolteacher and they had a daughter. I couldn't have wished for a better family to bring up my daughter and I have been sending them some of the money I earned from the proceeds of my bounty hunting days ever since.'

'I didn't know you have been supporting her financially but I've been to Nelsonville,' said John. 'It's a little coal mining town near to West Point but on the opposite side of the Hudson River. When I rode with General Morgan we raided it during the early part of the Civil War.

Luckily, we did little damage to the town; our target was the barges moored there. We burnt about ten of them.'

'Matt, does your daughter have a name?' asked Becky.

'They called her Lisbet as that was her mother's middle name. As I have never actually seen my child I don't know whether she takes after Anne in any other way,' said Matt.

'I haven't seen her either,' admitted John.

Their story brought Becky close to tears but her twin was more angry than sad.

'So what good will it do Lisbet if one of you is killed fighting over her past? Do you think she will thank the survivor for killing the other?' she demanded.

'No. Nevertheless, Miss Faith, I have already said, I've taken an oath sworn on the Sacred Book that my beloved sister, Anne, shall be avenged,' said John.

'Very well. If common sense cannot deter either of you, so be it,' said Faith.

Becky looked at her sister in astonishment. Never before had she known Faith to acquiesce so easily. She had known her sister put up a strenuous fight for things of far less importance, like the colour of a dress.

However, Becky had underestimated her sister for her twin had devised a plan. While the men slept in the bunkhouse, Faith joined her sister in her bedroom and began to explain it. As she did so Becky gasped for it was the most dangerous and audacious plan she had ever heard. So by playing devil's advocate, she tested her sister's resolve.

'Why should we risk our lives to save them from their own stupidity? After all, if John kills Matt, then might we not inherit the ranch? However unlikely that may seem, stranger things have happened in Texas.'

'True and although I might argue that if Matt outdrew Mr Wesley, we should be no worse off than before and the Bar-T would be denied the services of a man who is reputed to be one of the most deadly gunmen in Texas, would you want that, dear sister?'

'No, Faith, I would not. Unasked he came to my aid in my hour of need and then afterwards promised me his protection, for what reason I do not know.'

'Look into your mirror and you may see reason enough, my beautiful blonde-haired sister.'

Becky blushed at such a fulsome compliment from her much-loved sister but was too embarrassed to say anything. However, Faith continued after only the slightest pause.

'But what am I saying? God forbid that we should benefit from the death of someone so dear to . . . um . . . us,' she said blushing profusely as she corrected herself in an attempt to hide her ever-growing feelings for Matt from her sister.

However, her attempted cover-up was to no avail, Becky could read her sister's feelings as easily as she could read a book.

'You care for Matt!' she exclaimed.

Faith could not deny it.

'You think me very foolish to feel for such a man and one that I have only known only for a few days?' she asked instead.

Becky hugged her sister very tightly before replying.

'No more foolish than I who have known John for just a few hours,' she said.

86

Instead of scolding her sister, Faith merely smiled.

'Then my suspicions were also correct, dear sister. It seems that both our hearts have overruled our heads. But we must try to be serious for a moment. Apart from any feelings we may have towards our most notorious gunmen there is one other person who must be taken into our considerations, is there not?'

'Lisbet,' said Becky at once.

'Of course. Now let me go through my plan again. If it is to work then we must both act in perfect unison. Timing is everything. Each detail must be rehearsed time and again in our minds and every imperfection eliminated.'

Next morning, in spite of the forthcoming showdown, they all enjoyed a hearty breakfast. However, because the twins had spent most of the night rehearsing Faith's plan it was later than usual. So they had only just finished when they were interrupted by the arrival of Walt driving the old army wagon and Tom Johnson driving the twin's buggy. Although Tom did not yet know it, the return of the buggy was fundamental to the successful completion of Faith's audacious plan.

Tom had heard about the gunfight the day before and in spite of Matt's protests, refused to take any money for the buggy's extensive repairs.

'No, sir, Black Creek money is no good to me. Anyone who stands against the Bar-T deserves all the support I can give them. Believe me, although we are in the minority I ain't the only one in town who thinks that way. However, instead of payment, you could do me a favour. I need to take the old wagon back to Rockspring so that our young

Willard can take a load of supplies to his mother's home-stead.'

'Of course you can take it back. The mares used to belong to Willard's mother, didn't they?' asked Faith.

'They did. I guarantee that I will get them and the wagon back to you as soon as possible. In the meantime, I'll leave Trollop with you to pull the buggy.'

'That's another unusual name for a horse,' said Becky, unable to stop herself from giggling at the unfortunate sexual implication of the mare's name.

'Well begging your pardon, Miss Faith, and not wishing to be too indelicate, she's a mite too friendly with every stallion she meets and she will follow any man with an apple or carrot to spare.'

Tom and Walt had already eaten at Ma Cooper's. Her kitchen, regardless of the time, was never closed to her friends. So they refused breakfast but gratefully accepted several mugs of coffee expertly brewed by Becky.

Tom then went outside to tend the mares. Faith fol-lowed using the ploy that she needed to become acquainted with Trollop. Instead, she engaged Tom in earnest conversation. It seemed at first that whatever it was she wanted him to do did not meet with his approval. However, it didn't take Faith long to change his mind.

After the mares had been rested Tom and Walt began their journey back to Rockspring. It was the mares' fourth such journey in little more than twenty-four hours yet after their short rest they seemed almost as fresh as when they made their first trip. Nevertheless, as soon as they were out of sight of the ranch, the wagon halted and Tom dismounted.

'Wait here for my return,' he said to Walt and then headed back to the ranch on foot, taking care not to be seen.

It had been arranged that at the appointed time Matt would leave the ranch house and then walk slowly into the centre of the courtyard while John would do the same from the barn. As neither of them wished the girls to witness the showdown, they readily agreed to Faith and Becky's request to leave the ranch in the buggy and stay away until the gunfight was over.

7

SHOWDOWN - THE SISTERS TAKE ACTION

Noon. The appointed time for the showdown between Matt and John Wesley. Both men were so occupied in their preparations they barely noticed the girls as they drove slowly away in the buggy and paid even less attention to the direction they took.

For the first time in many years, despite their hitherto proven prowess with their six-guns, neither man was confident of the outcome of the showdown, such was the respect that each of them had for the other's ability. Yet unlike some other fast guns, Matt had no desire to prove he was the faster draw.

In truth this was a gunfight neither man really wanted. Yet there seemed to be no way out; John had vowed to avenge his sister's honour and Matt was determined to stay alive if only to support the daughter he had never met.

John watched as Matt opened the main door of the ranch and stepped into the courtyard. Only then did he leave the barn. Some twenty paces apart they stopped and faced each other.

'I'm sorry it has come to this, old friend,' said Matt.

'It was always going to end this way,' replied John sadly.

'If so, we should perhaps stand a little closer. Wounding each other will only lead to another showdown between us.'

'You are right Matt. Let death be swift and sure.'

'Then five steps forward, pause and then draw.'

'Agreed,' said John.

Slowly and carefully they both took, one, two, three paces forwards. . . .

Suddenly they were both engulfed in a cloud of blinding dust kicked up by Trollop as frantically pulling the buggy, she raced between the two would-be assailants.

Before they could react they were each almost bowled over by the sudden and fierce impact of a highly desirable female. Both men both reeled backwards only to discover that these female bodies had arms that hugged them so tightly, their gun hands were pinned to each of their respective sides.

Yet it was not Becky whose arms so forcefully embraced John, it was those of Faith, while her twin hugged Matt with all her might.

Trollop had been galloping too fast to stop so her driver, Tom, allowed the over-excitable mare her head and let her run round the back of the barn. The buggy slewed round, narrowly missing the bunkhouse and then drove back out onto the open range. Tom gave Trollop her head until she ran out of steam and then guided her to the creek and let her drink. When he thought she had drunk enough he drove the buggy back to where he had left Walt and then, as ordered by Faith, waited awhile.

Back in the courtyard, dust still obscured vision. Faith thrust herself in front of John, turned to face Matt and then put her hand behind her until her fingers firmly grasped the butt of John's six-gun. Becky did the same with Matt. As a result, neither man could draw.

'Matt, if you wish to carry on with this gunfight, you will have to shoot me first to get to John,' said Faith.

'And, John, you will have to shoot me first to get to Matt,' said Becky breathlessly. She had not judged her dangerous leap out of the buggy quite as well as her sister and the collision with Matt had knocked all the breath out of her.

At first, both Matt and John were too badly winded to reply; John recovered first but he was so taken aback by the twins' audacity he could hardly speak. However, it only took him a few seconds to recover his wits.

'Of course, I can't shoot you Miss Becky but what would you have us do?'

It was Faith, whose hand still firmly grasped his gun, who answered, 'For the moment, put aside your vendetta against Matt and join us all round the table to listen to my proposition. You too Matt, the proposition also concerns you. Then, if you still decide to carry on with this unnecessary feud, you can fight it out somewhere else. But whichever of you wins, don't bother to come back. Black Creek will have been sold to the Bar-T by then.'

Too stunned to speak, both men, covered in dust and their own confusion, meekly followed the twins into the kitchen. The coffee pot had been left on the hob and was still simmering so as usual, Becky did the honours. As she poured out the coffee John noticed her hands were still violently shaking.

'Now to business. John, you have pledged to avenge your sister's honour and it is a vow you feel you cannot break.'

'Yes,' he replied quietly.

'And to you that means you must face the man who you thought had deserted your sister in her hour of need.'

'Yes,' he replied again.

'So tell me, John, now you have heard Matt's side of the story, do you still think that he deliberately abandoned your sister?'

'No but. . . .'

'But me no buts, Mr Wesley. Instead, tell me honestly, if I offered you an honourable way out of your dilemma, would you take it?'

'Of course, Miss Faith.'

'Good, now we're getting somewhere. Matt, the offer I am about to make to John will require your consent, so listen carefully.'

'Faith, if anyone can find an honourable solution to end this vendetta without blood being shed it will be you and I for one will be forever in your debt.'

For a second she was taken aback by Matt's fulsome

praise but recovered quickly and began to outline her proposition.

'Firstly, Mr Wesley, you must agree to help us in our fight against the Bar-T.'

'Agreed. In fact, when you think about it, I've already started. There's one Bar-T gunman in Rockspring's Boot Hill as testament to that. But how does that solve my problem?'

'If – and it is a mighty big if – we win out against the Bar-T, then Lisbet is to come here and live with us. You have my word . . .'

'And mine too,' interrupted Becky.

'. . . that she will have the benefit of all the love and tender care which is in our power to bestow,' continued Faith as if Becky had not spoken. 'If she wishes she will be treated as our younger sister and this home will be as much hers as it is ours. To prove it she shall have half of my share of Black Creek.'

'And mine too,' interrupted Becky again but Faith had not yet finished.

'Matt, for his part, will undertake to carry out the responsibility to Lisbet that his situation demands. He has to agree to end his days as a bounty hunter and hired gun and take on the role of a loving father. Matt must also agree to continue to support her financially until the day she marries.'

'John, you have my sworn word that I will most willingly agree to all Faith's conditions,' Matt replied.

'But does this absolve me from my vow?' asked John doubtfully.

'I believe so, Mr Wesley, but in case you still have

doubts I have two further points to make. Firstly, last time I was in Rockspring I asked my good friend, Sheriff Foley, who also makes his living by using his ability with a six-gun, which of you is the faster draw. He told me that nobody knows since there is no discernable difference between you. Therefore, I ask you to consider one dreadful possible outcome of your gunfight; that neither of you survive. So then what would happen to Lisbet? Would not her future be one of toil or even worse? Indeed, tainted with the stigma of illegitimacy which back east will haunt her for the rest of her life, might she not turn to prostitution?'

'Without one of us to support and guide her, she might not have any choice about it,' said John, shocked by the thought.

'And what about Faith and Becky? What would their future be if we both perished in the gunfight?' asked Matt.

This time Faith could not help smiling warmly as she glanced at Matt. Nevertheless, she continued with her argument.

'My second point for you to consider, Mr Wesley, is how much better the life of your niece would be if she lived here on the open ranges of Texas. Here, in the Panhandle, men outnumber women by at least five-to-one. Consequently few of them are concerned by whether a girl is born out of wedlock. What I'm trying to say is that when the time is right, Lisbet is almost certain to make a more favourable marriage here than back east.'

'I go along with everything Faith has said except for one thing,' interrupted Matt. 'I believe it would be far more fitting if Lisbet's share of Black Creek came from me and not Faith or Becky. Then, if I was to slightly increase the twins' shareholding to eleven per cent each then between them and Lisbet they would own one third of Black Creek.'

As she looked at Matt another smile, this time only a little short of adoration, spread over Faith's countenance but she quickly suppressed her ever-growing feelings for him and again returned to the job in hand.

'Surely living here would be the best possible outcome for Lisbet. But it is a lot to take in all at once so perhaps, Mr Wesley, you might need a little time to think it over,' she concluded.

'Yes, I would like that. Perhaps, until noon tomorrow?' John said a little sheepishly, remembering that the noon just past had been the deadline for their showdown.

A few minutes later Tom and Walt returned. Without a word they unhitched Trollop and transferred the mare to the safety of the corral. Then, as if nothing had happened they set off for Rockspring in the wagon pulled by Daisy and Maisy.

Both Matt and John were still covered in the dust kicked up by the buggy as it raced between them. Unlike Matt, whose only change of clothes was his shabby old town garb, John always carried in his saddle bags an exact duplicate set of the clothes he normally wore. So he went to the barn to get them.

Becky gave him a few minutes to change and then followed after him. However, before he changed into his fresh clothes he sluiced himself down under the pump. As it was concealed behind the barn he stripped off and had only just put his pants and boots back on when Becky arrived.

Although his upper body was slim and sinewy rather than beefy, she could not help but notice that the muscles in his arms were extremely well defined. She blushed as thoughts of them wrapped around her naked body flashed through her mind.

But John's arms did nothing of the sort. Instead, he calmly put on his fresh shirt, buckled on his gun belts and only when he had satisfied himself that the holster and the six-gun in it were perfectly positioned again did he acknowledge her presence.

'That was a damned crazy stunt you pulled. You might have been badly hurt jumping out of the buggy like that. What were you thinking? In that cloud of dust I might have shot you by mistake thinking you were Matt.

'He's a lucky man though; you must think an awful lot of him to put yourself between him and my Peacemaker. Yet why your sister, charming though she is, should decide to shield me, I've no idea!'

'John Wesley, how could you be so stupid! I've still got your short-barrelled Peacemaker but luckily for you it's back in the ranch house. Otherwise, I'd probably save Matt the trouble and shoot you myself.'

Becky was not as quick to anger as her slightly older twin but when roused she was just as formidable.

'Miss Becky, I'm sorry to cause offence; it's just that I've never met anyone quite like you or your sister for that matter. But you have me all confused. I know you two stopped the gunfight yet I am at a loss; I don't understand why you took such a terrible risk.'

Becky's anger evaporated as quickly as it had come. Yet she noted that John had stopped using his old fashioned way of speaking and guessed that meant he was indeed very confused. If so, she was not above teasing him a little.

'So you like my sister then, do you, John? Because from where I stood it seemed you were enjoying her embrace just a little too much! Should I be jealous? I ask because after she threw herself into your arms, you have gone back to calling me Miss Becky.'

'No Miss Becky, I didn't mean to suggest that your sister had any special feelings towards me or I for her. It's you and you only I care for.'

He hadn't meant to say anything about the feelings he had for her, after all they had only met yesterday. Yet Becky's actions had him so flustered the words just tumbled out of his mouth. Far from being affronted by his familiarity, Becky was delighted.

'So why haven't you kissed me properly yet?' she asked boldly.

'I, um, well. . . .' he spluttered until Becky relented and stopped teasing him.

'John, dearest John. I threw myself at Matt because I didn't want to believe that you would deliberately shoot me. As for you shooting me by mistake in the dust cloud, I was never worried about that. I believed you to be a man of honour so I knew you would not seek to gain an advantage over your opponent by firing at him when he couldn't see you. Was I not right?'

'After knowing me for only twenty-four hours you think that highly of me,' he said, finding that difficult to believe.

'John, I could say so much more but instead I shall most certainly shoot you if you don't kiss me this very instant and start calling me Becky and only Becky.'

He did both but she liked the kissing better.

'John,' she said as she at last pulled away, 'I know that the feud between yourself and Matt is a matter of honour. In spite of my wanton behaviour towards you I too have principles and so will not gainsay my sister. If you decide to carry on the feud then, though it breaks my heart in two, this will have been our last kiss.'

Utterly amazed and yet delighted by her boldness John was at a loss for words. However, having started to reveal her true feelings, Becky was not.

'Since I am to be deprived of offering half my shares to your sister I have one other offer to make, providing you stay.'

'And that is?' he asked, his voice full of puzzlement.

'Me – or rather my body. Anytime, anywhere and I will never say no to anything you want. Then, when you've had enough of me, you're free to ride away. So will you have me until then?'

For several seconds he said nothing. Then pulling himself together he gave her a surprisingly measured response.

'No,' he said to her utmost disappointment. 'Your sister was right. Now I know that my niece is still alive and that Matt knew nothing of my sister's pregnancy, to continue the vendetta would be wrong. Apart from making her life worse than it already must be, shooting Matt now would make me no better than my hypocritical father. In church he preaches love, forgiveness and tolerance yet in his private life showed none of those qualities towards his own granddaughter.'

'So you will stay and help us against the Bar-T?' she asked breathlessly.

'Yes. Nor will I risk breaking your heart by leaving Black Creek, unless of course, you tell me to go. As to your offer, wonderful though it is, it wasn't necessary. I had already decided to stay.'

'I'm so glad; yet my offer to still stands.'

'Then I shall most certainly make love to you in every possible way, should one day you decide to marry me. But as we've known each other for no more than a day, take your time to decide. Get to know me a little better first; always remember what I am, a hired gun and bounty hunter just like Matt used to be.'

'John, are you proposing to me?' she said, her voice quivering with emotion. Yet she feared his answer above all, believing that she must have misunderstood him.

'Two days ago, I didn't know you. In truth I was just a hired gun looking for vengeance. Then I met you and everything in my life changed. Now all I want is to settle down with you if you will have me. Of course, that will have to be sometime in the future.'

'Oh!' she gasped.

'Becky, I have said too much too soon. So take as long as you need to decide, I'm not going anywhere.'

'Nor am I, my love. Yes, you are a hired gunman and a bounty hunter just like Matt used to be. Indeed, he was an outlaw until the Governor pardoned him. Yet despite his past, Faith has feelings for him. Indeed, I believe her to be as much in love with him as I am with you. If his past does not bother my sister why should your past deter me?'

'Because the past has a habit of catching up on a man like me. I have earned my reputation of being a fast draw the hard way. By that I mean I have outdrawn everyone who drew against me. So now there's always someone somewhere looking to prove he's faster than I am.'

'Then he will have to get by me first, Remember, I've still got the little six-gun you gave me. As to the rest, when we first met you spoke so strangely I was scared of you. But that soon passed and now I'm only scared of losing you. As to anything else, I've already said so much about my own feelings you must think me terribly forward and little better than a bar-room floozy.'

'Becky, I think no such thing. Indeed, I have nothing but respect for the way you and your sister have tried to run Black Creek.'

'Nothing but respect? What you just said about our future together led me to believe that you felt much more than that about me,' she said teasingly and smiled in that special way he could not resist.

'You know I do, but you know that any future we may have together must wait until we have settled our account with the Bar-T.'

She couldn't help it – she was in his arms in an instant. He had said our account.

8

PRELUDE TO RANGE WAR

While Becky and John were sorting out their future, back in the ranch house a similar if more animated conversation was also taking place.

'If you ever do anything as stupidly dangerous as that again Faith, I'll lock you in your bedroom and throw the key away.'

She looked at him beguilingly.

'Fine, just so long as you stay in the bedroom with me.'

'Faith, will you be serious for a minute. Jumping off the buggy at the speed it was going, it's a wonder you or your sister were not maimed or killed.'

'Well Matt, how else were we to stop you killing each other?'

'Faith, I hope that you never have cause to do anything as dangerous again. As to the showdown between John and me, I fear that in spite of you and your sister's bravery and your plan for reconciliation, you have only postponed the inevitable. That said I don't doubt that John will aid us against the Bar-T. After that. . . .'

'After that, if he has not already changed his mind, he will have it changed for him, although not by you or me,' replied Faith mysteriously.

'Then by whom? I don't understand,' said Matt.

'Of course you don't, you're a man,' she replied equally mysteriously.

No matter how much Matt quizzed her about what she meant she would not be drawn further. Instead, she changed the subject.

'What do you think the Bar-T will do next?' she asked.

'Nothing until Trench thinks his herd is safely out of the way on the trail to Dodge and he has all his gunmen back at the Bar-T.'

'What then?' she asked.

'Well, when he discovers that John has sided with us he might then try to hire another top gun to replace him. On the other hand, he has at least sixteen hired guns so should he realize that there are only the two of us, he might try an all-out assault on Black Creek.'

'Well, I can shoot a bit. Before the trouble with the Bar-T blew up I used to go out on the range and shoot enough jack rabbits to keep the pot full for most of the week.'

'Jack-rabbits don't shoot back but the Bar-T gunmen will and it's a cinch bet that at least some of them will be crack shots with a rifle or carbine. If you were hurt or even worse killed I would never forgive myself.'

'I wouldn't be too pleased either,' replied Faith dryly. 'But it's my home too. I won't give it up without a fight and I'm sure that Becky feels that way too!'

'Faith, I don't expect you to give up without a fight, but the truth is that however good John and I are with our six-guns we don't have enough fire power to successfully defend the ranch.'

'So what can Becky and I do to help?'

'Learn to reload our Winchester carbines and six-guns in as little time as possible. That should enable us to almost double our fire power.'

'Will that be enough?' asked Faith doubtfully.

'I'm afraid not. Even with double the fire power there are only two of us. But if I were in Trench's position I would opt for a siege. If he does we might hold them off for a little while but eventually we would have to sleep. In any case, although we have plenty of fresh water, sooner or later we are going to run out of food – or worse still, ammunition.'

'We've only the ammunition you and John have brought. So what happens if we do run out?' asked Faith, horrified at the thought of being at the mercy of Trench and his Bar-T gunmen.

'We make sure that doesn't happen,' said John. He had been standing in the doorway arm-in-arm with Becky as together they listened to Matt's summing up of their situation. And together, hand-in-hand this time, they entered the kitchen. Faith was not slow to notice the change in their relationship.

Over dinner, it was John not Matt who outlined their strategy.

'First, we must stock up,' he said and then added, 'of course; getting more food supplies is important but obtaining as much ammunition as we can carry must be an absolute priority. As Matt said, we don't want to run out in the middle of a siege, do we?'

'No, replied Faith, 'but we only have the buggy. I know it has been repaired but it's still rather frail. Apart from the high cost of purchasing the ammunition, boxes of it are very heavy. I'm afraid that they and more food supplies may again prove too much for the buggy.'

'So we will have to make more than one trip,' said Becky. 'As Faith is a much better shot than me I am the least valuable here should the Bar-T attack. So it makes sense that I be the one to drive to town and get what we need. I'll travel by night and have the buggy loaded up during the day and then drive back to the ranch during the next night.'

'Not alone you won't,' said Faith grimly. She was thinking of the gunfight between Matt and the Bar-T gunmen when she last visited Rockspring.

'Although it means leaving Matt as the lone gunfighter defending Black Creek, I'd be happy to accompany Becky,' said John.

Faith noted with some satisfaction that John's use of Becky's christian name brought no reproof from her sister. However, she was quite shocked to find that she relished the idea of being alone in the ranch with Matt. Nevertheless, she didn't want to appear too eager so she remained quiet.

'I have been told the Bar-T is putting every kind of pressure on the owner of Rockspring's store not to supply

Black Creek but he may think twice about refusing to serve me, especially as I have enough money on me to pay cash for the ammo,' said John.

'Does that mean you're going to stay and fight?' asked Faith, breathlessly.

'Yes,' replied John.

'And the vendetta?' she asked even more breathlessly.

'Now I know all the facts about my sister Anne's fate and if Matt agrees, then it's over for good. Besides, I now have someone worth fighting for,' John replied.

Hearing John's words Becky blushed deeply. Faith immediately noticed her sister's change of complexion. Matt did not and thinking John was referring to his daughter Lisbet, stepped forward and proffered his hand.

'I never wanted to draw against Anne's brother,' he said.

Aided by the light of a full moon, Becky, in the buggy pulled by Trollop, set off for Rockspring just after midnight. Much to her disappointment John chose to ride Cochise. However, she had to admit his reasons for doing so were good ones. Firstly, the stallion needed the exercise and on horseback John could scout the trail ahead of them. Also by riding Cochise the amount of weight then carried by the buggy would be lessened, reducing the likelihood of it breaking down again.

Even by moonlight, Trollop pulling the empty buggy should have been capable of making the trip in well under four hours. However, if Becky couldn't have John riding beside her then she planned on a romantic interlude somewhere along the trail.

Any such thoughts that Faith may have harboured towards a similar sort of dalliance with Matt were soon dashed.

'Faith, my best guess is that the ranch will be safe until at least dawn. So get some sleep until then. Who knows when we will get another full night's sleep?'

Reluctantly she had to admit Matt was right. However, she had another idea.

'Matt, you can't defend the ranch from either the barn or the bunkhouse so I think you should move your things into the house. The bed in the room next to mine is all made up.'

She tried to make her idea sound no more than just common sense but there was absolutely nothing she could do to stop her heart racing while he thought over her plan – or seemingly skipping a beat when he agreed to move in.

'You're right, of course. I had thought about it but reckoned you wouldn't want your reputation to be. . . .'

'Better my reputation be a little bit tarnished than lose the ranch because you have been consigned to the bunkhouse,' she interrupted.

In spite of what she may have secretly desired, her honour remained untarnished. Although she quite deliberately left her bedroom door tantalizingly ajar Matt made no attempt to enter.

They kept careful watch all through the next day but there was no sign of Trench or any Bar-T gunmen. Nor was there any trace of either Becky or John the following night.

At first Faith was not concerned by her sister's absence,

believing that during the night her bolder and more forthright sister had enjoyed better fortune with her romance with John than she had with Matt. But as noon came and went, she began to become more concerned. Sensing that concern, Matt sought to comfort her.

'John is more than capable of taking care of any Bar-T gunmen they might have encountered in Rockspring. You may have forgotten that when you were discussing his rank of captain he told you that he had fought for the Confederacy under the command of General Morgan when they raided Nelsonville.'

'Yes, I do remember,' said Faith.

'What he didn't tell you was that although the raid was a success, the General's army was ambushed and all but two hundred were either captured or killed. John and General Morgan were among those who were captured and sent to a Yankee prison. The General, John and four others were the only ones to escape but then John got separated from the rest. Nevertheless, he somehow managed to travel safely through hundreds of miles of Yankee territory until he eventually reached the Confederate Army. So I guess getting your sister and the supplies back from Rockspring would pose him few problems even if they had to veer off the trail to avoid any Bar-T gunman.'

'You think that's what happened to them?' asked Faith.

'Possibly but it's more likely they have been delayed by a problem with the buggy or perhaps they just waited for the old army wagon to return from Willard's mother's homestead.'

Whatever the cause for the delay, there was no sign of Becky in the buggy or John riding Cochise that day.

Although Matt and Faith took it in turns to stand watch the following night there was still no trace of her twin or John.

There was something else puzzling Matt. By now the Bar-T herd should have become used to a daily routine as they began the long trek northwards to Dodge. Even so, at this early stage of the drive there was always danger of an unguarded action or unexpected noise spooking the herd into a stampede. So the last thing the cowhands, usually about fifteen in number, needed were the Bar-T gunmen in close proximity to the herd.

Matt had expected that Trench would have sent at least some of them to raid Black Creek, if only to discover how well it was defended. Yet there was no sign of them. So what else was Trench up to?

9

REINFORCEMENTS

The answer to Matt's question arrived next day. In the middle of the morning a wagon slowly approached the ranch. However, it was not the old army wagon but a much larger prairie schooner. It was clearly heavily laden because it was being pulled by no fewer than six horses. Even from a distance Matt could see it had three occupants, none of whom resembled Becky or John.

As the prairie schooner came nearer Matt called Faith to his side. It was not long before they could see it was being expertly driven by the huge Tom Wilson. Walt, acting as guard, was clutching a shotgun; sitting in between them was Ma Cooper.

As the prairie wagon entered the courtyard they could see it carried another passenger. About forty, she wore men's riding boots; her long muscular legs, very tightly encased in snug-fitting trousers hung erotically over the rear of the prairie schooner. Her long hair had clearly been dyed blonde. From her blood-red lips dangled a black cheroot and in her arms she carried a huge Sharps buffalo rifle.

'This is Susie, my partner and protector,' said Tom.

Susie alighted from the rear of the prairie schooner with an agility that belied her size. She was one big lady; close on six foot tall and her muscular body must have weighed almost two hundred pounds. Yet there was not an ounce of surplus fat on her. She eyed Matt provocatively, as her gaze went from his boots to the top of his head.

'Pretty boy, ain't he?' she said addressing Faith. 'But don't you worry none, Miss Wilson, he's all yours. I like my fellows to be big like my Tom. Why, I'd wear your fellow out in no time at all. Though it might be fun doing so,' she added as an afterthought.

Faith was too startled to respond.

'Bar-T gunmen raided Rockspring and burnt down the property of anyone they thought had helped Black Creek,' said Walt.

'Burnt my place down to the ground,' said Ma Cooper bitterly. 'The bastards left me homeless and then afterwards laughed about it. So Miss Faith, I hope you will be wanting to hire a good cook.'

Although Matt owned most of the ranch he looked at Faith quizzically.

She responded immediately.

'Mrs Cooper, of course we need a cook. For the moment I'm sorry to say we don't have any money to pay you but you can stay here as long as you need to.'

'Thank you kindly Miss Faith. A roof over my head and

a bed to sleep in is all I need but call me Ma, everyone does.'

Faith led them into the kitchen, Ma and Tom followed closely behind but Susie hesitated.

'Seeing that I used to be a saloon girl it don't seem right for the likes of me to go mixing with respectable folk like you,' she said.

Faith burst out in peels of laughter.

'Susie, Matt was once a notorious outlaw and my sister has been out on the range for the last two nights with another infamous bounty hunter and hired gun. So come in and sit down, while I make coffee for all of us.'

'No you won't, Miss Faith. May as well start off as I mean to continue, so I'll brew and serve the coffee,' said Ma Cooper firmly.

While she busied herself doing just that and examining the kitchen at the same time, the others sat round the table. It seemed Tom had a tale to tell.

'Willard set off to his mother's house in the old army wagon but arrived at the same time as some Bar-T gunmen. He put up a fight but got shot up for his troubles. They then threw Mrs Smith off the homestead and burnt it down. They left her the old wagon to get Willard back to Rockspring. I guess burning down the homestead and shooting the deputy was intended to be a warning to anybody in town who might be thinking of siding with us and challenging the Bar-T.'

'Was Willard badly hurt?' asked Faith anxiously.

'No, the first shot was a flesh wound. Although he lost a lot of blood, he will be fine. But his days of being a deputy are over; the second shot that hit him made a mess of his gun hand.'

'Maybe that's no bad thing, I don't think the boy was cut out to be a law officer,' said Matt.

'Mr Johnson, have you seen my sister?' asked Faith anxiously.

'Yes, last time I saw her she was fine, but I've more to tell before I come to her part of the story.'

So Faith had to wait for news of her sister while Tom related the rest of his tale.

'As soon as Willard was made comfortable and Mrs Smith had been found a place to stay, Sheriff Foley rode to her homestead to check out the damage. Then, just after he left, Bar-T gunmen rode into town and started acting as if they owned it and that's where your sister enters the story.

'You see, rather than risk overloading her buggy I suggested that after I had cleaned it up – Willard had lost a lot of blood – she should switch back to the old wagon.

'Your sister left her buggy in my stables and with Mr Wesley went to Ma Cooper's for a meal. Then all hell broke out; the Bar-T gunmen raided my stables and burnt it down; the old wagon and your buggy were destroyed in the blaze. Luckily, most of my horses were either out being exercized or managed to escape from the fire of their own accord. Susie and me hid in my brother's office until the gunmen left town.'

'So what happened to my sister?' asked Faith anxiously.

'She and Mr Wesley were eating at Ma Cooper's when the Bar-T gunmen raided it. Their mistake! Mr Wesley killed one and wounded another as he got your sister and Ma Cooper out of harm's way. But instead of going after him, the gunmen burnt down Ma Cooper's place.'

'Lost most of my pots and pans; the few I managed to save are in the prairie wagon. Maybe it's just as well seeing how old most of the pans are here,' said Ma Cooper sternly.

'But what happened to my sister?' Faith asked impatiently.

'On her way here by now, I guess. As soon as the Bar-T gunmen left she and Mr Wesley started to look round for replacement wagons while I went to round up my stray horses. Where your sister got the prairie wagon from I don't know but when I got back it was already loaded. I harnessed my horses to the wagon while Walt fetched Ma Cooper.'

'Why did my sister not come back with you?' asked Faith.

'She and Mr Wesley went to collect another prairie schooner. Why? I don't know; the one I'm driving could carry as much weight as your buggy and the old army wagon combined,' replied Tom.

After the coffee break was over and while Ma Cooper busied herself in the kitchen, Walt tended the horses and Matt and Tom unloaded the prairie wagon. Only one other buffalo rifle had survived the fire but Tom had managed to get a few boxes of shells for it and the one belonging to Susie. Unfortunately the storekeeper, Mr Bridger, had refused to supply any other ammunition.

They had just finished unloading when another prairie wagon as heavily laden as the one they had just emptied approached the ranch. However, this was being hauled as if it were no more than a toy by the two carthorses, Daisy and Maisy.

Tom was delighted to be reunited with his fine mares; he feared they must have been lost when the stables were burnt down. Much to the delight of her sister, driving them with surprising ease was Becky. By her side, toting two six-guns and carrying a Winchester carbine was Tom's brother, Sirus. At his side was a tattered old case stuffed to the brim with papers and what looked like old parchments. Riding guard to the prairie schooner on his copper-coloured roan was John.

'Sorry we've been so long, but as you can see we have a new recruit,' said Becky pointing at Sirus.

'I had some legal work to finish and some papers I had to find before I could leave Rockspring. I haven't had time to study the old parchments closely yet. Unfortunately, most of them are in Spanish and my knowledge of that language is very limited. However, I have been able to determine that there are several references to this ranch. But whether or not they have any relevance to today, as yet I have no idea,' said Sirus apologetically.

'If you think they may be of some importance it might be as well to keep them under lock and key in the safe,' said Faith.

'Yes,' agreed Sirus. 'Call it a hunch, for I've little else to go on but Trench was awfully interested in them even though he doesn't speak a word of Spanish.'

'While we were waiting for Sirus I used the time to persuade Bridger to let us have the ammunition we needed,' said John. 'He was a bit reluctant at first but a six-gun in the hands of a gunslinger with a reputation like mine soon changed his mind. In the end he agreed to supply the ammunition for free and even offered to give us more supplies provided we didn't use his store again.'

'John can be very persuasive. I think if we had stayed five minutes more Mr Bridger might have given us the whole store,' said Becky, grinning from ear to ear.

'Maybe,' said John breaking out into a rare smile. 'Of course, I realized that we already had enough supplies to keep us going for some time. However, as Black Creek seems to be gaining more recruits and courtesy of Mr Bridger, these supplies are free. So we brought back several sacks of flour, a sack of coffee beans and umpteen cans of beans as well as the ammunition.'

'Where did you get the prairie schooners?' asked Tom.

'Courtesy of the Bar-T,' replied John, smiling broadly. 'When I realized they had a stable in Rockspring I paid them a visit and asked if we could borrow them.'

'There was nobody at the stables to object. Except for the prairie wagons it was completely deserted. Even their stable horses were gone,' laughed Becky.

'How did you manage to find Daisy and Maisy?' asked Tom.

'Didn't have to. As soon as the fire was put out they came back to your stable of their own accord,' replied John.

'But after burning down my stables, why would the Bar-T then abandon their own stable?' asked Tom.

Nobody had the slightest idea.

For the last year Black Creek's corral had been occupied by only one old hack, the steed the twins had used to pull the buggy. Now it was also home to Geronimo and

Cochise, Daisy and Maisy, the six horses that pulled the first prairie schooner to arrive at the ranch and of course Trollop. Whilst there was plenty of room for all of them in the corral, there was only enough hay to feed all of them for a few days.

So it was agreed that Geronimo and Cochise should be stabled in the barn while the rest of the horses were to be taken down to the creek and left to roam. As the best grass grew along the creek and round the lake there was little likelihood of them straying.

Black Creek now had nine residents yet its large kitchen did not seem unduly overcrowded. Far from being despondent over the loss of her home, Ma Cooper was in her element as she cooked the evening meal for all of them.

While she did so the men not only unloaded the second prairie schooner but carried the surplus food stores into the barn and then hid them under the straw.

Over dinner the men wanted to discuss how best to defend the ranch but were prevented from doing so by an animated discussion by the women over sleeping arrangements. Indeed, the discussion became so heated they almost forgot the men were also in the kitchen.

'It's quite simple,' said Faith, 'we've five bedrooms, one each for us girls and as Matt has already moved into one of the bedrooms, he can stay in the ranch house. The rest of the men will have to sleep in the bunkhouse.'

Led by her twin sister, there was a chorus of objections to her plan. Becky was not about to allow Faith to have Matt in the next bedroom to her while John slept in the bunkhouse. However, she knew she could not win using

117

her feelings as the basis of her argument, so she tried another tack.

'If the ranch house is attacked during the night, without help Matt wouldn't be able to protect us and defend the ranch house at the same time,' she said defiantly.

Susie was more forthright.

'Night comes and there's a big old Texas moon shining, then I want a man to lie beside me in the hay. Your barn will do fine for Tom and me. Besides, if the Bar-T men get into the barn they could isolate you people in the ranch from the bunkhouse.'

'She's right on both counts. I'd be heading for the barn too if the man of my choice had got the gumption to ask me,' said Ma Cooper looking hard at Walt, but he avoided eye contact. Rescue from his embarrassment came from an unlikely source.

'I'm a decent shot but it will need at least two of us to guard the bunkhouse so I need Walt with me,' said Sirus.

Further lengthy discussions followed and so it was not until the end of the meal that the sleeping arrangements were agreed by all. Then, the immediate priority was to get everyone concerned settled down in their new quarters. As this also involved moving sufficient munitions to the barn and the bunkhouse to enable their new tenants to defend themselves against an all-out attack, there was no time left to discuss battle tactics.

After refusing any help Ma Cooper set about the washing-up. However, it was clear that the events of the day had taken their toll on her strength. So while Becky showed John to his new abode Faith insisted on helping

118

out with the dishes. Afterwards, it was Ma Cooper's turn to be escorted to her new bedroom. When she saw how large and comfortable it was, she broke into tears.

'Fancy me getting to stay in a place like this,' she said between her sobs.

'You can live here for as long as you have a mind to,' said Faith.

10

UNDER ATTACK

The Bar-T came at dawn, but not to fight for there were only six of them. Under the safety of a white flag Trench rode into the courtyard while his men remained safely out of rifle range. Or to be more precise, out of range of any Winchester rifle.

Trench did not dismount, nor did he offer the traditional greeting. Instead, he got straight to the reason for his visit.

'Miss Wilson, if you wish to save unnecessary bloodshed, please step into the courtyard. You have my sacred promise you will not be harmed.'

During his life Trench had broken his promise, sacred or otherwise, so many times his oath had absolutely no value. But this one time he actually meant to keep it.

Hesitantly, Faith did as she was bid.

'Mr Trench, what do you want at this early hour?'

'To offer you one last chance to leave this place in

120

safety. To avoid unnecessary bloodshed I will make one last offer, doubling the value of my first one. I will now pay twenty cents for each and every acre of Black Creek. The money will be paid into your bank as soon as my herd is sold at Dodge. Until then, you and your sister are to be my guests at the Bar-T.'

'As your offer also involves my sister I will have to consult with her before giving you my answer,' replied Faith.

'Then fetch her out here,' Trench ordered.

Trench's demand took Faith by surprise. For the briefest of moments she hesitated but recovered almost instantly.

'My sister is not accustomed to rising as early as this,' she lied.

'Very well Miss Wilson, I am not an unreasonable man. It so happens I have some urgent business in Rockspring that requires my immediate attention. So you can have a little time to discuss my new offer with your sister.'

'Thank you, you are most generous,' said Faith, barely keeping at bay the sarcasm in her voice.

However, Trench was too blown up with his own self-importance to notice it and mustering all the menace he possessed, carried on as if Faith had not spoken.

'But remember this, Miss Wilson; if the pair of you don't show up at my ranch by dusk tonight, I shall take that to mean you have declined my latest and final offer. Take my advice and accept it; one way or another I will have Black Creek so let me assure you that if you refuse it will take a lot more than a couple of hired gunmen, no matter how good they are, to save your ranch.'

121

With that Trench turned his horse around, dug his spurs deep into the flanks of the unfortunate beast and galloped furiously back to his men. Within seconds, they too were on the move as they all galloped away in the direction of Rockspring.

Faith watched them ride away, then still visibly shaken by her ordeal, she walked back into the ranch house. What she hadn't known was that during her ordeal she had been much safer than she had thought; for from the main room windows of the ranch house the guns of Matt, John and Sirus had been trained on Trench, all ready to fire had he shown the slightest sign of treachery.

Faith had faced Trench on her own because Matt had asked her to do so. Over a cup of steaming hot coffee she asked what had been gained by her masquerade.

'Time and knowledge,' said Matt.

'We now know that we have at least a day before Trench can begin his attack,' said John.

'And we also know that Trench is not aware that Tom and Sirus have joined us.'

'You are forgetting me,' said Susie. 'With a carbine I can shoot straighter than most and some of those who tried to force their way on me against my will have felt the cutting edge of my bowie knife. And in northern Texas I joined up with my buffalo gun.'

'You mean you were a buffalo hunter,' exclaimed Becky.

'Shot a few 'til I came to my senses. Thirty buffalo hunters, some of them earning over a hundred dollars a day and not another white woman within fifty miles. Fifteen dollars for two hours was my fee and some nights

I earned almost as much as some of the buffalo hunters did during the day.'

A stunned silence met this revelation until Tom began to laugh.

'Don't be shocked, that's how I met Susie,' he said.

'You were a buffalo hunter?' asked Becky again.

This time it was Susie who laughed.

'No, Tom was the buffalo hunters' farrier and he also repaired and maintained the wagons that carried the hides to the railhead.'

'Each buffalo hunter paid me a dollar a day to look after the spare horses and maintain the wagons. As there were thirty of them I did all right for myself,' said Tom.

'You can say that again,' said Susie. 'Tom was so good in bed he had me begging for more. So I only charged him five dollars for the first time each day and nothing for each occasion afterwards and that was something he managed to do quite often!'

Again there was a stunned silence in the kitchen. Then John broke the mood.

'I think we are straying from the subject. Now we have a good idea what Trench will do next, what are we going to do about it?' he asked.

'First, we get the ladies as far away from Black Creek as possible. Then we prepare ourselves for a long siege,' said Matt.

'Matt Crowe, you once said you would go down on your knees and beg if I would stay on at Black Creek. I told you then that the ranch was and will always be my home. Do you think I'm going to leave it now when its very survival is threatened by the Bar-T? Besides didn't you say that you

123

needed me to reload your guns?'

'Yes, I did,' admitted Matt, 'but. . . .'

'But nothing,' interrupted Becky. 'Texas wasn't only founded by Austin and Sam Houston's army. It was also fought for and won by the settlers whose wives fought side by side with their men against the Mexicans and then the Indians. John said he would stay on and fight for Black Creek and if he and all of you don't yet realize it, he's going to be my man so I'll be fighting by his side, too.'

'I ain't no lady like Miss Becky nor am I a settler's woman. But Tom is my man so like the women settlers of old I will also fight beside my man. Besides, I've a score to settle with the Bar-T. Those bastards burnt my home and means of earning a living down,' said Susie.

'If siege it be, then you will need someone to cook your meals and keep an eye on how much food we have left. So I'm staying here too and if necessary I will fight for my new home if I can borrow a shotgun. Never forget those Bar-T bastards burnt down my home too,' said Ma Cooper vehemently.

Matt looked at the four very determined women and saw that this was one argument he was not going to win.

'Very well ladies, you've argued the points most cogently, so welcome to the Black Creek army. But you must all be prepared to take orders, is that understood?'

'As Matt outranked me in the Confederate Army he is best suited to lead us,' said John.

The women all nodded in agreement.

'In that case John, you're my second-in-command. As such, should anything happen to me, the responsibility of looking after the twins and Lisbet will be yours. Do you agree?'

'Me, be a rancher? As a last resort only. But thou hast my word should the worst befall thee, then I will always look after the girls to the best of my ability,' replied John, slipping back into his old manner of speech.

Certain that the Bar-T would strike next day, Matt went over his plan to defend Black Creek. But it was not that which kept him awake to the early hours of the morning. No matter how he tried he could not get Faith out of his mind. . . .

The Bar-T, or at least a dozen of its gunmen, attacked next morning. They planned the raid to coincide with the time they thought that the inhabitants of Black Creek would be enjoying their breakfast.

In two by twos and best cavalry fashion, the gunmen galloped into the courtyard. Half of them peeled away and rode behind the barn, meaning to attack the ranch house from the opposite side. But in doing so they had to ride past the front of the bunkhouse.

As they did so, Tom, Susie and Walt opened fire. Unfortunately, a man riding a galloping horse does not make an easy target, no matter how near he may be. Even so, they might have done better had they not aimed high to avoid hitting the horses.

Although one of the riders was winged, only one other shot struck its intended target. Hit from close range by a bullet from Susie's very powerful Sharps buffalo rifle, the unfortunate Bar-T rider was quite literally blown out of his saddle and crashed against the back of the barn. Not that he felt any pain; he was already dead.

Three of the surviving riders peeled off and rode round the back of the barn and the bunkhouse but circled round the back of the empty corral and past the side of the ranch house. Their purpose being to attack it from what they expected to be its undefended rear.

Undefended because they assumed that John Wesley must have been shooting at them from the bunkhouse and Crowe would be kept fully occupied dealing with their fellow gunmen who were making a full frontal attack on the ranch house.

They had not thought that the sisters would actually shoulder arms but marshalled by Ma Cooper, they stood poised at the kitchen window. All three women were armed with double-barrelled shotguns.

Far too casually, the Bar-T gunmen dismounted and tethered their horses. Then, they drew their six-guns and strolled towards the kitchen door.

Ma Cooper fired first. Faith was only a split second behind Ma Cooper as she too fired both barrels of her shotgun. Only Becky held her fire. She had been instructed to do so by Matt; her function being to provide cover for the other two women while they reloaded their shotguns.

It wasn't necessary, although in truth Ma Cooper had opened fire fractionally too early. If she had waited just ten more seconds the approaching gunmen would have been literally ripped apart by the buckshot. But they were just a little too far away for that to happen. Nevertheless, the gunmen reeled backwards under the impact of the buckshot. Their flesh torn apart and covered in blood, the appearance of the gunmen was so frightful both sisters began to retch.

It had the opposite effect on Ma Cooper. Indeed, she would have fired at them again but Becky would not let her have the other, still loaded, shotgun. Not that it mattered, there was no fight left in these three Bar-T gunmen.

However, things were not going quite as well at the front of the ranch house. Although Matt and John had each accounted for one Bar-T gunman, Sirus had been hit in the chest. Luckily, it was only by a ricochet so the power of the bullet had been almost spent by the time it hit him. Nevertheless, he was in no fit state to continue fighting. Sickened by the carnage she had helped to create at the rear of the ranch house, Faith found some atonement by tending his wound.

'Matt, what's our next move?' asked John.

'We sit tight. We have food and fresh water a plenty so while it's quiet, would you check how things are in the kitchen and if it's all right, get Ma Cooper to cook us breakfast.'

'What about Tom, Susie and Walt?' asked John.

'Assuming they're all right, I hope they will stay where they are. As long as they stay in the bunkhouse they should be safe enough.'

Half an hour later, apart from Becky, they were all eating sausage wrapped in bacon and as many fried eggs as they wanted. She and John watched out through the slatted windows for the Bar-T gunmen but that did not stop John from enjoying a second helping of bacon.

'John, the carnage makes me feel sick so how can you eat after all the bloodshed?' she asked.

'Too easily, my darling girl. You see, a very long time ago, I felt as you do now and in truth I wish I still did. But even though I survived, the war and its battlefields change a man. It hardens his soul so much he no longer even remembers the way he used to feel. In fact, long time survivors like me and Matt feel absolutely nothing.'

Unbidden, a tear or two leaked from Becky's eyes as she began to realize what he must have seen and been through.

'Of course, from the moment I met you, dear Becky, all that changed.'

Not for the first time she was in his arms in an instant but this time he had a plate of bacon in his left hand (thus keeping his gun hand free) and so could not hold her properly. It mattered not for the vigour of her embrace locked them together.

Becky's boldness almost cost her life for at that moment a fusillade of shots was aimed at the ranch house, some of which penetrated the slats that only partially covered the windows, narrowly missing her head before slamming into the wall opposite the window.

'Everybody hit the deck and stay down,' yelled Matt as more bullets tore through the window slats and buried themselves into the far wall.

The barrage continued but the only danger to the prone occupants of the ranch house was from flying splinters of wood dislodged from the slats by the fusillade of bullets. Then, as suddenly as it had started the firing stopped, to be replaced by the sound of horses as they galloped away. Suddenly, there was a single shot followed by a distant cry and then for several moments, complete silence until. . . .

'Hey! You in the house! You can come out now, the varmints have skedaddled,' bellowed Susie.

Matt took Faith's hand and helped her to her feet. He was pleasantly surprised to find that she continued to hold his hand after she had got to her feet. Ma Cooper made her way over to the injured Sirus. In order to examine his wound she began to loosen his tie and undo his shirt.

He had been extremely lucky. The almost spent bullet had only glanced against his ribs. So there was no blood, just an ugly bruise marked the spot where he had been hit. Nevertheless, Sirus felt as though he had been hit by a sledgehammer.

'You can get up now,' said Faith disapprovingly as she noticed that her sister was not only lying on the floor with John on top of her but she was clinging to him so tightly he was unable to get up.

As she slowly scrambled to her feet, Becky noted that her sister had not let go of Matt's hand. Nor did she show any indication of doing so.

Although the wall on the other side of the room to the windows had at least three dozen bullets embedded in it, the only real damage was to the window slats and they had been shot to pieces.

The damage to the would-be attackers was far more severe. At the back, outside the kitchen door, lay two Bar-T gunmen; their bodies mutilated by buckshot. They had bled to death. Two bodies lay in front of the barn, shot by Matt and John while the body of a fifth gunman slain by Susie slumped in front of the bunkhouse.

The men began the grisly job of searching the bodies before loading them into one of the prairie schooners. They made an interesting discovery; each dead gunman had two fifty-dollar gold pieces on him, the rate Trench was willing to pay for the destruction of Black Creek.

They took the money, five hundred dollars in all, plus all the ammunition the five dead gunmen were carrying. They also took one shotgun and four Winchester carbines and added them to their growing arsenal.

Matt then let Geronimo and Cochise out of the barn. As Geronimo had not been exercised for some time, Matt rode him down to the creek. On his way he passed the body of another Bar-T gunman, also the victim of Susie's buffalo rifle. The dead man also had two fifty-dollar pieces in his pocket. Matt removed them and then began to search for horses to pull the prairie schooner. He didn't have to look far. Daisy and Maisy, seemingly oblivious to the recent mayhem at the ranch house, were too busy munching the rich and lush spring grass near the bank of the creek to have wandered off.

Not for the first time, Walt drew the short straw and had the job of driving the prairie schooner and its grisly cargo to the undertakers at Rockspring. It was the unanimous opinion that with his badly bruised chest and possibly having a cracked rib, the last thing Sirus needed was the long and often bumpy ride to Rockspring. So a temporary bed was rigged up in the study. It also contained the safe but Sirus was prevented from studying the old Spanish parchments he had brought with him from Rockspring by the non-stop attentions of the womenfolk.

Over a late evening meal Faith asked what Matt

intended to do with the money they had taken from the dead Bar-T gunmen.

'Keep it. Once our troubles with the Bar-T are over, we shall need every dollar we can lay our hands on to get Black Creek up and running again.'

'Is keeping the money legal?' asked Becky.

'Probably not,' admitted Matt.

'On the other hand, if Trench lodges a complaint to the circuit judge that we had taken the money from the bodies of his men, wouldn't that be tantamount to admitting he paid them to attack Black Creek?' said John.

'So what do we do next?' asked Faith.

'Nothing. After today's fracas Trench will know he has a fight on his hands if he wants to get hold of Black Creek. Don't forget that all told we must have accounted for about half of his gunmen,' Matt replied.

'True,' replied John, 'but we had the element of surprise on our side this time. It may not be so easy next time.'

'John, after losing so many men I can't believe they would risk attacking us again,' said Becky.

'The questions to ask are why did they attack the ranch in the first place and why did they chose now?' asked Susie shrewdly.

'Everybody knows the Bar-T needs our water and they raided us now because they thought there were only Matt and John to protect the ranch,' said Faith.

'I reckon you think me to be nothing more than an old saloon whore but them answers don't make sense to me,' replied Susie.

'Susie, there are no saints here. I have already told you

131

that you are one of us so I won't have you talking yourself down like that,' said Faith sternly.

'Amen to that,' said John, 'but Miss Susie, I would like to know why you think Faith's answers to your questions don't make sense 'cause they seemed pretty good to me.'

Susie blushed deeply to think that she was being taken seriously. However, that did not prevent her continuing.

'Miss Faith, you said the Bar-T needed water for their cattle and we've already established that Trench believed there were only two men defending Black Creek. So why didn't his men drive the steers not required for the cattle across our range and down to the lake? I ask the question because without leaving the ranch house unguarded, how could Matt and John have stopped them?'

'You're right, we couldn't have and no matter how deadly they may be at close range, any six-gun is not that accurate at long range. So any advantage Matt and I might have over the Bar-T gunmen would have been nullified out on the range,' conceded Matt.

'In that case, why did Trench pay his men an extra one hundred dollars to attack the ranch house?' asked Faith.

'To get his hands on the old parchments I brought from Rockspring and destroy them,' said Sirus, pain etched all over his face as he staggered into the kitchen.

11

THE QUIET BEFORE THE STORM

Next day, the horses including Trollop were rounded up and returned to the corral. Then, using the water stored in the tank in its roof, Matt and John thoroughly soaked the outside of the ranch house.

'Just in case the Bar-T think of using fire arrows to burn the ranch house down,' they explained to the womenfolk.

It was two days before Walt and Tom returned from Rockspring, during which time the Bar-T gunmen were conspicuous by their absence. Once again the prairie schooner was heavily laden but oddly, it also contained most of the personal effects of Sheriff Ben Foley.

'Trench has forced an emergency council meeting. He wants them to vote Ben out of office,' explained Walt.

'Why would Trench do that?' asked Faith.

'Once Ben is out of the way, Trench will put forward his

own man,' replied Walt.

'If he succeeds we won't get any more supplies from Rockspring,' said Faith as she recollected how two Bar-T gunmen had tried to stop her entering the town's only store.

'That's why last night we stuffed the prairie wagon full of everything we could lay our hands on,' said Tom.

Tom was right. Apart from the sheriff's personal stuff, which included a bow complete with a quiver of arrows, the prairie schooner contained enough provisions to last another three weeks. It also contained three dozen boxes of ammunition for the six-guns and Winchesters and a box full of the special ammunition used by buffalo rifles. And that was not all, for tucked under some sacks at the rear of the prairie wagon were several sticks of dynamite. The latter were stored very carefully in the barn.

Although extremely painful, the injury to Sirus proved to be no more than very bad bruising that severely restricted his movements. However, that was not the source of his frustration. Some of the most important parchments he had removed from Rockspring were very old, written in script and in a language that was unknown to him. Others were written in old Spanish and yet bore the unmistakable signature of Sam Houston. There were only a few words he could translate but among them were Black Creek; the ranch's name appeared in several parchments including the one signed by Sam Houston. But why? Sirus had no idea but knew someone who might be able to decipher them. However, first there was the little matter of the Bar-T to attend to, although after the mauling their gunmen had received at the hands of Matt and John, perhaps they were not quite as formidable as they used to be.

If Sirus thought that Trench was in any way deterred by the loss of his gunmen he was sadly mistaken. The following day Ben Foley arrived at the ranch with news and all of it bad. Firstly, he had been voted out of office although he had agreed to continue as sheriff until a replacement had been found. The delay had been caused by Susie on the day of the raid; the gunman she had shot as he rode away from Black Creek had been Trench's intended new sheriff.

If possible, the second part of Ben's news was even worse. Not only had Trench sent a telegram to his agent to hire a top gunslinger to act as sheriff but he had also requested a dozen replacement gunmen. They could only have one purpose; the total destruction of Black Creek.

Once again, over a late evening meal, they discussed the latest developments.

'Well, we've fought them off once, we can do it again,' said Faith.

'I doubt they will try a full-scale attack on the ranch house again,' said John.

'Why not?' asked Becky.

'It's like I said before,' interrupted Susie. 'If the Bar-T wanted to, they could drive their steers to our water right now and without leaving the ranch house almost defenceless, what could we do to stop them?'

'Except this dispute is only partly to do with water rights. I can't translate much from the old parchments but I can just make out that there is something else behind Trench's attacks on Black Creek but as to what it is, I have yet to discover,' admitted Sirus.

'Given that he will soon be in control of Rockspring I think Trench will do nothing until his new gunmen arrive. Then, he will probably cordon off the ranch and wait us out,' said Matt.

'I believe you're right, especially as he may not know about our last two loads of supplies,' said John.

Over the next few days a sort of false calm descended over Black Creek. Ben returned to Rockspring only to find that two new deputies had been appointed in his absence. Both were Bar-T men and it seemed that Trench had offered to pay their wages. An offer readily accepted by the town council. As this made Ben's position as sheriff untenable, he resigned. As soon as he had completed all the necessary paperwork and collected the rest of his belongings, he returned to Black Creek.

Matt thought Ben's arrival combined with the improvement in the condition of Sirus tipped the balance of power in favour of Black Creek, although only until the next batch of Bar-T gunmen arrived. In the unlikely event that they too were defeated Trench would simply hire more gunmen to replace them.

As long as the Bar-T ranch stood it was clear to Matt that there could be no peace for Black Creek. *Stood*; the word flashed again and again through his mind. Then it came to him; apart from being more than useful with a six-gun, Ben had one other special talent that, when he had served under Matt during the Civil War, he had used to great effect. Utilized now it might be enough to end the range war in Black Creek's favour. So that evening he outlined his plan.

'I'll need to practice, been some time since I used my bow and even then I'll need to compensate for the extra weight,' said Ben.

'Take a couple of days. After the mauling we gave his last raiders I don't think Trench will do anything until all his new gunmen have arrived,' said Matt.

Next morning was also peaceful. As Matt had predicted there was no sign of Trench or his remaining gunmen.

After breakfast Black Creek became a hive of activity. While Becky gathered eggs, Sirus studied the old parchments and Ma Cooper busied herself in the kitchen. Tom used his handyman skills to build much stronger shutters for the windows and Susie moved their things out of the barn into the spare bedroom.

John kept lookout while Ben began to practice. He had hardly used his bow since the Civil War but during that bloody campaign, many a Union sentry had silently been struck down by an arrow fired from it.

Faith had other things on her mind.

'Matt, I want to check the cows at the far end of the lake; some of them should have calved by now.'

'Fine, but just to be on the safe side I'd better come with you,' he replied.

His reply was just what Faith had secretly hoped for. So midmorning they set out, Faith on Trollop and Matt astride the magnificent Geronimo.

The lake was bigger than Matt realized and by the time they had reached its far end the ranch house was out of sight. But the slight risk was worth it for as far as the eye could see were groups of heavily pregnant cows contentedly grazing by the water's edge. Dotted in among them, suckling at the mothers' teats were newly born calves.

'They always come here to calve,' said Faith. Her voice was full of wonder for although she had seen it many times before, she never tired of seeing the annual miracle of birth.

Matt on the other hand was more interested in the brands carried by the cows. As they slowly rode among the cows he noticed that most of them carried the Bar-T brand. However, here and there were a few carrying the Black Creek mark. Of course, the newly born calves were unbranded and that gave Matt an idea.

'If the births go well, in a couple of years' time there should be enough steers to form a good sized herd, although I've no idea how to drive such a herd north to Dodge,' he admitted.

'But won't the Bar-T claim the calves as their own?' asked Faith.

'Not if we brand them first,' he replied grimly.

'Do you really think we can defeat the Bar-T?' she asked.

'Yes, Faith, I do. But then I thought the South would defeat the Union,' he added ruefully.

Distracted by the efforts of a newly born calf to stand up for the first time, Faith didn't answer. Instead, she dismounted intending to give the calf a much-needed hand. However, accompanied by much licking and encouraging moos from its mother, the calf struggled to its feet of its own accord. Then, although it could hardly stand upright it immediately searched for its mother's teats and began to suckle.

Matt also dismounted and knowing that both horses

would be too content grazing on the lush spring grass to wander away, dropped their reins.

'What a wonderful thing nature is,' said Faith as she braved herself to ask the one question which had been on her mind ever since she first realized she was in love with Matt.

'What about you Matt? I know I'm looking far into the future but once the herd you were talking about has been sold and the money is in your bank, will you still want to be a rancher?'

His silence scared her more than the Bar-T's raid had ever done. But he was only carefully thinking out his answer. Outlaw and gunman he might have been, but he too was a little afraid he might say too much or too little. Most of all he feared that she would feel out of obligation to him to give an affirmative answer to the one question that up to now he had not dared to ask.

'Yes Faith, I want to make Black Creek my home. But I want you to understand that whatever I feel, you are under no obligation to me whatsoever. You are free to live your life in any way you choose and. . . .'

'Matt, shut up and kiss me.'

He did just that. Not once but twice until gasping for breath, she broke away.

'The answer is yes,' she said when she had recovered.

'But I haven't asked you anything,' he replied, utterly bewildered.

'Oh yes you have, even if you are afraid of the words. So my answer is yes. Matt, of course I will marry you.'

12

RANGE WAR BREAKS OUT

A few minutes before dawn, a breeze suddenly sprung up. Into it a strangely misshaped arrow whistled through the air, but weighed down by the burden it was carrying plunged into the ground perhaps ten paces short of its intended target, the Bar-T ranch house. Seconds later a second arrow followed; although it carried a little further, it too fell short. So it clattered to the ground to be enveloped by the same gloom that now hid the first arrow from Matt and John. They were positioned behind a massive cactus some fifty yards away from Ben and Susie.

'Got to get nearer. I hadn't reckoned on this damned breeze,' mouthed Ben to Susie.

On all fours, they slowly inched their way forward but in doing so left all semblance of cover behind them. Nevertheless, not until Ben was confident that he was in range did they stop. Unfortunately, by that time the sun had begun its daily ascent into the heavens. It would only be a matter of moments before its rays heralded the new day leaving Ben and Susie in full sight of the ranch house.

Susie carefully passed another arrow to Ben who with equal care transferred it to his bow. Taking aim was not easy due to the stick of dynamite attached to it. Ben pulled on the bow string with all his might before letting go and this time the arrow struck its intended target, the ranch house roof. Unfortunately, it didn't take hold and slid noisily down the sloping roof on its way to the ground.

Confident that no one would dare to attack the huge Bar-T ranch, its occupants had not posted guards or sentries and in spite of the noise created as the arrow fell off the roof, no one in the ranch house stirred.

Ben shot his fourth arrow and then cursed out aloud. He had over-compensated and the arrow struck the top of the ranch house chimney stack, lodging in a position that made the stick of dynamite attached to it almost impossible to hit.

Susie, still crouched on the ground, handed the fifth and last but one arrow to Ben. Hands chilled by the breeze he fumbled and it dropped to the ground. Fortunately, not with enough force to cause the dynamite to explode.

As always the neckline of Susie's blouse was cut so low it left little to the imagination. As she bent forward to retrieve the arrow absolutely nothing was left hidden from Ben's view.

Seeing the startled expression on his face and then

realizing the reason for it, Susie smiled. With her free hand, she took hold of John's hand and guided it down the front of her blouse until it reached her nipples.

'Just for luck,' she whispered as she let go his hand.

It was probably no more than a coincidence; the fifth arrow struck true and embedded itself in the roof.

'Save the last arrow – if this doesn't work we may need it to defend Black Creek,' mouthed Ben.

Susie acknowledged and reached for her Buffalo rifle. In doing so, she again quite deliberately exposed almost all of her breasts. Then, at a signal from Matt, hidden from the Bar-T by a clump of house-high cacti she took careful aim and then fired at the arrow stuck fast in the chimney stack. At the same time, Matt and John using their Winchester carbines fired at the arrow embedded in the roof.

At first nothing happened. Matt feared that his scheme was not going to work. Then, the stillness of the early morning air was rent by a violent explosion emanating from the chimney. It seemed that Susie's aim had been true. What caused the delay in the explosion was never found out.

Flames shot skywards as what was left of the chimney stack collapsed and fell through the hole blasted in the roof. This was instantly followed by a series of eruptions all round the ranch. The formerly imposing building was instantly engulfed in flames and smoke.

Satisfied that they had done enough damage, Matt waved to Ben and pointed to where they had tethered their horses. Unfortunately, horses being naturally gregarious enjoy the company of others of their kind. So much so they will almost always greet other horses with a series of friendly but loud whinnies.

To avoid their own horses neighing a greeting to any of their kind kept in the Bar-T corral and thus warning any guards, Geronimo, Cochise, Trollop and Ben's horse had been tethered out of sight behind a clump of huge cacti, approximately half a mile away from the ranch house.

Matt cursed at his mistake. As a former military officer he had taken for granted that lookouts or sentries would have been posted to protect the ranch house. But there had been none so they could have ridden much closer. As it was they now had to cover on foot half a mile before they could begin their ride back to the comparative safety of Black Creek.

Worse still, Ben's failure to hit the target with his first few arrows and the need to get closer to the ranch house meant not only that the raid had taken longer than Matt had planned, but Ben and Susie had to run much further than he had planned to get back to the horses.

Of course, they had approached the ranch house under cover of darkness but the rays of the rising sun meant they were now fully exposed. Unfortunately the ground was not only uneven, the few cacti between them and those behind which the horses were tethered were too small to provide any cover.

Running any distance in riding boots encumbered by rifles and carrying boxes of ammunition was a tough enough task for the men but proved to be especially difficult for Susie. Not only was her large and curvaceous body not designed for speed she was also carrying the last remaining arrow and her buffalo rifle. As it was much

143

larger and far heavier than the men's Winchester carbines it was no surprise that after a hundred or so paces she began to fall behind. Then, completely out of breath, she had to stop.

Realizing she had stopped, Matt whirled round expecting to see the Bar-T gunmen in hot pursuit or a host of hostile rifles trained on them. Neither was the case. Not only was the Bar-T ranch house ablaze, sparks from its roof, in spite of the adverse early morning breeze had still managed to carry to the bunkhouse. The lack of rain had dried out its wooden structure so it was no surprise that it too was on fire.

Consequently the Bar-T men who had been sleeping in it were more concerned about rescuing their possessions than chasing after the raiders. From their uncoordinated actions Matt could only conclude that Trench had either been killed by the dynamite blasts or his business affairs meant that he had spent the night in Rockspring. He was only partly right for it was not business alone that had delayed Trench's return to the Bar-T.

Thick black smoke then completely blotted out his view of the ranch house. Of course, if Matt could not see the gunmen through the smoke then the gunmen couldn't see him or any of his companions.

The smoke got steadily thicker and blacker. A further series of violent explosions shook the ground. Matt thought the fire must have reached the Bar-T's ammunition store. That distraction combined with the thick smoke not only gave Susie time to get back her breath but allowed all of them to head for their horses at a more leisurely pace.

*

There was no jubilation over the destruction of the Bar-T ranch and bunkhouse that evening. Rather, an air of uncertainty pervaded the kitchen of Black Creek. Had Trench been sleeping in the ranch house at the time of the attack? If so he must have been killed by the explosions. Yet Matt could not rid himself of the idea that if Trench had been there, he would have ensured that lookouts would have been posted.

Trench was not the only thing on Matt's mind. Somehow, he had gotten engaged, if that was the right term, to Faith. Did he love her? Of course, almost from the first moment he met her. However, being a ranch owner was one thing but getting married and then becoming a father was something entirely else. He was a gunman with a reputation second to none; not even John Wesley had a worse one. What sort of legacy was that for a child to inherit?

John had no such qualms about his future with Becky. Long ago he had learned to live for the day and let the morrow bring what it may. He was certain that Trench had not been on the Bar-T ranch at the time of their raid. Therefore, John's concerns lay with how best to defend Black Creek against what he considered to be an inevitable revenge attack. John was damned sure it wasn't going to be Black Creek that went under. For once, the range war was personal; this time he had someone special and she was worth fighting for.

In spite of his best efforts, translating the old parchments had proved beyond Sirus. Mostly they had been in

Spanish and his knowledge of that language was not that good. To make matters worse there were also passages in most of the parchments written in a language he had never encountered before. But he knew someone who might have; an old lawyer, mentor and friend who occasionally supplemented his income by translating old documents. Sirus had consulted him several times when as a very junior lawyer he practised law in Austin.

Unfortunately his old friend had retired and now lived by the coast near Galveston. To get there would take many days of hard riding across the vast wastes of the Texas Panhandle. For the moment his badly bruised ribs ruled out such an arduous trek. Besides, his guns were needed at Black Creek.

The men and Susie (she absolutely insisted) took turns to stand watch but only the arrival of Bridger disturbed the peace. He had news and all of it was bad. For helping Black Creek, he had been run out of town by Bartholomew Trench and his henchmen, the two new deputies. Trench had been in town for several days. His agent had sent a telegram advising him that several new gunmen were due to arrive in Rockspring within the week.

They had actually arrived the day before yesterday but instead of immediately riding to the Bar-T they stayed at the Alhambra to fully enjoy the 'hospitality' of the saloon girls. Never one to miss out on a good time, Trench had also spent at least one night in the arms of one of the saloon girls.

Bridger then explained why he had elected to ride to Black Creek.

'I expect you don't remember me, Major Crowe,' he said, 'but during the war I served in your unit for a few months. Then I got I got wounded. Before they ran me out of town I overheard Trench bragging to his new men how they were going to burn down Black Creek. I thought you should know. Being an enlisted man I never carried a six-gun during the time I fought for the South but I'm as good as the next man with a rifle. So here I am, ready to take your orders just like I used to do.'

In truth, although Matt had thought Bridger had looked familiar when he first met him, he had little recollection of the store man serving under him during the Civil War. Nevertheless, Matt accepted his offer of help and then began to formulate another plan to thwart the Bar-T.

13

BLOOD OVER BLACK CREEK

It was not until some time after Bridger had arrived at Black Creek that Trench and his newfound allies set off for the Bar-T. Their trip took longer than usual because Trench decided to circumnavigate the Black Creek rather than take the more direct route across its ford. Consequently it was almost dusk before they arrived at the Bar-T only to find that the ranch house had been burnt to the ground and the bunkhouse had been gutted.

Trench was in turn shocked and then blinded by an uncontrollable rage. For the first time in his life he acted impetuously and after rounding up all his remaining gunmen, he then promised them and his new recruits five hundred dollars each to burn down Black Creek.

So early next morning they headed for Black Creek. In spite of the anger which burnt deep within him, Trench was in no hurry to get shot. It was not that long since the little ranch had easily rebuffed a frontal attack by his gunmen. So during the long night spent in the barn, the only one of his buildings not to have been burnt to the ground, he had devised a new attack plan.

However, he formulated his plan on the incorrect premise that although they might have a little help from the twins and maybe Walt, Black Creek had only two experienced gunmen to defend it. No matter how good they were, Trench was confident that they would eventually be overwhelmed by the sheer volume of the gunmen at his disposal.

He was quite wrong on both counts.

Although the land immediately surrounding the big Bar-T ranch house had offered little cover for Matt and his raiders, the Panhandle between the Bar-T and Black Creek was uneven, full of dry gullies and ridges. It was from the top of one of these ridges hidden behind some rocks that John observed the cavalcade of Bar-T gunmen as they passed below him at little more than walking pace.

It had been his idea to scout the area around the Bar-T's ranch house and he had left Black Creek long before dawn to do so. It didn't take a mastermind to work out that Trench and his gunmen were headed for Black Creek although he had no idea why they were travelling at such a leisurely pace. He waited until he was sure he could not be seen, then rode Cochise at full gallop back to Black Creek.

This time, rather than sit back and wait for the Bar-T to attack the ranch house Matt intended that they should mount a daring counter strike and finish the range war.

149

Within the next few hours his daring plan must succeed or else he, John and Ben would be dead. In that case, what future could there be for Faith and Becky? He shuddered to think.

Aware that the dust cloud kicked up by a large number of galloping horses would be seen from the Black Creek ranch house, Trench and his men approached the ford at little more than walking pace. This caused the riders to bunch tightly together making them an unmissable target.

From the crest of the ridge upon which Matt had first viewed Black Creek, came first one then another shot. In spite of the distance the bullets from the two buffalo rifles struck home. Before the Bar-T riders could recover Matt and John leapt out of the long alfalfa grass in which they had been hiding and emptied their carbines into the riders.

Overhead, an arrow sped – only to be struck by a well aimed bullet. The dynamite the arrow was carrying exploded instantly. Although it flew too high in the air for the explosion to cause much injury the gunmen's horses were startled by the sudden noise. Chaos reigned supreme as the Bar-T riders desperately tried to control their steeds and get out of the line of fire. Some of them dashed downstream only to find that as soon as the ford ended the creek became so deep their horses had to swim for all they were worth. Consequently their riders were in no position to return the fire of Sirus and Bridger whom Matt had positioned a little downstream to cover the riders' escape route.

A few riders did manage to get past them only to be cut to ribbons by the combined shotgun fire of Walt, Bridger, Faith and Becky. Indeed, their blood turned the otherwise crystal clear waters of the creek deep red.

'Trench, you didn't tell us that Crowe had a bloody army,' snarled one of the newly recruited gunmen as he threw his arms up in the air in token of his surrender.

The rest of the surviving gunmen threw their weapons into the ford before raising their arms. Realizing there was nothing else he could do, Trench also surrendered.

The battle had lasted no more than a few minutes. Only a few Bar-T gunmen and Trench remained uninjured. On the other hand, no one from Black Creek had received so much as a scratch.

'Mr Crowe, what are you going to do with us?' asked one of the still mounted gunmen.

'Nothing. I too was once a hired gun. All I need are your solemn promises that that you will ride straight out of this Territory and never come back,' said Matt.

The gunmen instantly agreed and moments later the only trace left of them was the dust cloud kicked up by their galloping horses. Trench, however, was made to dismount and his hands were then tied behind his back.

'John, while we take Trench back to the ranch house, better get the girls away from the creek,' said Matt.

His dreams of empire and political ambition thwarted forever, it was a crestfallen Trench that was forcibly led to the ranch house. As all the others left, John made his way to the twins who were standing on the bank of the creek looking at the mangled bodies of the gunmen and their blood as it flowed down the creek.

151

Faith turned away but Becky remained transfixed, seemingly mesmerized by the appalling scene of dead and dying men, the blood from their bodies turning the creek red.

John put his arm around her.

'Dearest Becky, there was nothing else we could do. Come away from the bank and try to forget all that you have seen this terrible day.'

'No, John. Let me stay a while. I played my part in this massacre. I never want to forget the sight of the bodies and the blood flowing down the creek for that's what it cost to save Black Creek.'

Nevertheless, John managed to persuade Becky to leave the bloody battle scene and escorted her back to the ranch house. Ma Cooper, the only one not involved in the battle had hot soup and even hotter black coffee waiting for all of them except Trench, who was locked in the barn.

There was still much to do. John organized the round-up of the bodies, helped Walt and Tom load them into one of the prairie wagons and then after a shower went to find Becky.

Accompanied by Ben, Walt and Tom set off in the prairie wagon for Rockspring. Ben was sure that several of the dead gunmen featured in what used to be his file of wanted posters. Although he didn't want his old job as the sheriff of Rockspring back he was determined to ensure any reward money was claimed. He knew a charming widow and her son Willard needed the money to start over again. Unless, of course, she would let him look after her on a more permanent basis. Well, now he was no longer sheriff, there was nothing to stop him asking, was there?

Faith asked Susie to stay at the ranch but at first she declined.

'Look, you know what I'm like around men, especially when Tom's not around. I wouldn't want Becky to think I was trying to take her man away from her,' she said.

'He's not my man and in any case I guess now the trouble with the Bar-T is over he will soon be on his way,' Becky said sniffily as she flounced out of the room.

She was quite wrong. John had overheard part of the conversation and went after her. He stopped her on the porch.

'When we first met, did I not promise thee that I would protect thee and all that thou held dear?' he asked her.

'Yes, you did and have done most honourably. But the danger has gone, hasn't it?' she replied.

'And you want me to go too?' he asked gently.

'No, John.'

'I need you to be sure. I am what I am, I can't alter my past or bring back to life those I've shot.'

'Of course not. But I killed today in cold blood and I find that I don't regret it. So we are two of a kind.'

'If that's what you think, perhaps you would do me the honour of marrying me?' he said nervously.

'Would we stay at Black Creek?' she asked.

'For as long as you wish.'

'In that case my darling man, my answer is yes and as you once said that you wouldn't make love to me until after we married, the sooner the better.'

In the kitchen another kind of meeting was taking

place. With the danger over, Sirus had decided to ride to Galveston to see if his friend could translate the old parchments. However, from the little he had managed to decipher he needed power of attorney over the Bar-T but Trench refused.

'If everyone else would like to take a little walk, I need to have a little chat in private with the man who ordered the burning down of Tom and my stables,' she said.

They left Susie alone with Trench, although at first he was openly defiant.

'What's an old-time whore like you going to do? Strip and scare me to death with that old body of yours?' he scoffed.

'That's mighty foolish talk considering you're tied up and I've got this,' Susie said brandishing her bowie knife. 'By the way did I ever tell you about the time I entered a buffalo skinning competition? Didn't win it, finished second. Got a trophy though, a silver chalice. You will have to take my word for it 'cause it got destroyed when your men burnt my home down.'

A cry of pure terror echoed throughout the ranch house followed by: 'I'll sign, I'll sign. Just keep this she-devil away from me.'

It was Trench. However, Susie wouldn't say what she did that scared Trench so much he signed every piece of paper put in front of him without even reading it. Then, in spite of his still badly bruised chest, Sirus immediately rode to Galveston taking the parchments and the papers Trench had signed with him.

The owner of the Bar-T was then transported to

Rockspring to stand trial. Any hope he might have had of being sprung from jail evaporated when the two deputies whose wages he was paying resigned and high-tailed it out of the Territory. Tom and Walt were then appointed temporary deputies.

It was six weeks before the circuit judge visited Rockspring. Trench's trial followed a few days after his arrival. Trench was charged with causing Tom's stables and Ma Cooper's home to be burnt down as well as being responsible for ordering the destruction of the Smith homestead. He was found guilty on all these charges but because of insufficient evidence, acquitted of the murder of Mr Smith. A long prison sentence might have been his fate had he also not been found guilty of rustling Black Creek cattle. He was hung two days later, the time it took to build the gallows.

Life at Black Creek began to return to normal but not for long. News of the sale of their cattle included in the Henderson herd meant that the little ranch was solvent again. So a telegram was sent to Matt's daughter, Lisbet, inviting her to come and live at the ranch.

To Matt it seemed an age before the reply was received but in reality it was only a few days. Not only was Lisbet's answer in the affirmative but her guardians agreed to escort her, providing they were well compensated for their troubles.

Matt agreed. It was to be a long journey for such a young girl. First by carriage to New York and then by sea to the port of Galveston where Sirus, his business with the parchments concluded, would be waiting for her.

Lisbet's sea cruise led to an interesting development. A

number of cowboys joined the ship at St Louis and amongst them were four who had been part of the Bar-T cattle drive to Dodge. They were Quakers so instead of spending their money in the gin parlours and saloons of that notorious town, they had travelled by train, albeit by a circuitous route, to St Louis and then by pure chance boarded the same steam ship that Lisbet and her guardians were already on.

They soon struck up a friendly relationship with young Lisbet. Of course they knew Sirus from his dealings with the Bar-T so when they docked at Galveston, the cowboys were glad to take up his offer of employment.

Sirus purchased mustangs for them and a chuck wagon in which to carry supplies for the long trek across the Panhandle to Black Creek. Lisbet refused to ride in the chuck wagon and demanded a pony of her own, although he had some misgivings; riding hundreds of miles across the wild open spaces of the Texas Panhandle was a very different proposition to riding in the verdant countryside around Nelsonville. However, in spite of her tender years Lisbet proved to be an accomplished rider, even riding her pony across the mighty Pecos River unaided.

Her arrival at Black Creek caused Matt to act in a way that even surprised Faith.

Barely able to keep the tears from flowing, he addressed her in a voice full of emotion.

'Welcome to Black Creek. I would have known you anywhere; you look just like your mother when she was your age.'

As the cowboys settled into the bunkhouse, there was a celebration dinner taking place in the ranch house. It went on long into the night but it was not until Lisbet was settled into her new bedroom that Matt began to quiz Sirus about hiring the cowboys.

'Matt, before I explain about the cowboys, my fee for my professional services and expenses incurred is a little over one hundred thousand dollars.'

'But you know Black Creek doesn't have that sort of money,' protested Faith and Becky in unison.

'Besides what could you have been doing that cost so much money?' asked John.

'Sometimes when it is necessary to obtain a satisfactory and quick solution to what might have otherwise been a lengthy and tricky legal problem it is necessary to dangle a few carrots before those you need to act favourably towards you,' replied Sirus.

'There speaks a true lawyer, but I haven't the faintest idea what you're talking about,' admitted Tom.

'In plain words, Sirus means the money has been spent bribing people,' said Susie.

'Not bribing. Just making people see what was best for Black Creek was also best for them,' replied Sirus mysteriously.

'Enough is enough,' interrupted Matt. 'Sirus, please explain in a way we can all understand.'

'It begins with those old parchments. I had them translated and they date from the beginning of the Texas War of Independence; things were going pretty badly for Texas until the Mexican garrison stationed at Rockspring was taken by surprise and captured. A deal for their release ceded most of the land around here to the leader of the guerrilla army that had captured the garrison. That leader was the grandpa of Faith and Becky.'

'So that's how we came to actually own Black Creek,' said Faith.

'Not just Black Creek but all the tens of thousands of acres beyond it. In fact, almost all the land now known as the Bar-T,' said Sirus.

'But are the parchments still valid? Would they stand up in a court of law?' asked Matt.

'Trench thought so. Remember his claim to the Bar-T range was the Texas way; an announcement in the newspapers that he now owned it.'

'A claim backed up by his gunmen,' said Susie.

'Yes, but now they and Trench are gone. Thanks to Susie's powers of persuasion Trench signed a legal document renouncing his claim to the land. As it was witnessed by the sheriff of Rockspring, there could be no doubt about its authenticity. Then, when I was in Galveston, I lodged a claim to the Bar-T on Matt's behalf.'

'Why? It's not as if we need the land,' said Becky.

'Our claim was not just for the land but for the Bar-T brand and the two thousand head of cattle that were in the holding pens at Dodge. I cut a deal with the bank and they withdrew their claim to the herd providing we paid off the debts run up by Trench from the proceeds generated by its sale.'

'Was there enough money to do that? Apart from anything else, keeping twenty or so gunmen on the payroll must have cost a small fortune,' said Becky.

'Yes. But it doesn't end there; Trench also owned the Alhambra saloon as well as the only stables left in Rockspring so now they both belong to Black Creek.'

Peace returned to Rockspring. Susie was put in charge of the Alhambra saloon while Tom took over the running of the stables. Bridger was then reunited with his store. Ben took up Matt's offer and became Black Creek's top hand.

Lisbet took to life on the ranch as if she had been born there and was delighted to act as bridesmaid to Matt and Faith's and John and Becky's joint marriages.

The Bar-T ranch house was never rebuilt as both couples elected to live at Black Creek. Apart from the magnificent views, Ma Cooper's cooking was too good to miss.

As Black Creek began to lay claim to the Bar-T range, Ben led the newly hired cowboys as they planted markers denoting the eastern boundaries of the combined ranches. Then, they began the task of rounding up the cattle on the old Bar-T range and legitimately this time, they drove them to the once again crystal clear waters of Black Creek.